KDRAMA QUEEN REIGNS

By Donna-Lynne Hanlon

Dedication

Since this series deals a great deal with Angelique Randolph's relationship with her mother and birth father, it is only fitting that this is dedicated in loving memory of my parents, Ethel and Donald Hadfield. While they are nothing like the characters in the story, they were and remain an inspiration and driving force in my life. You are sorely missed but forever in my heart.

Acknowledgements

My list of people to thank grows longer as this series progresses. I extend my sincerest gratitude to the following people for their contributions to this endeavor.

To all who wrote to me to encourage me to continue Angelique's journey through multiple upheavals in my personal life including a major relocation and job change. Thank you for your patience.

To Stacey Kaufer and Kim Trang Nguyen for taking the time to read the manuscript and offer suggestions and for being my biggest fans as well as my editors.

To the past and present members of my Korean Culture Club, K-Kin, a new generation of fans that keep me young at heart.

To all the artists from the songs and OSTs from all the KDramas mentioned in the novel whose music provided the 'feels' that I wanted to capture while writing different chapters.

And, always, to my Lizzy Girl who took me down the 'Rabbit Hole' of KPop, KDrama, and KCulture which provided the spark for these writings.

Kamsahamnida!

Disclaimer: This is a work of purely speculative fiction. It is not intended to infringe on any rights by and of the companies and/or individuals involved in the production of any series mentioned here.

TABLE OF CONTENTS

EPISODE 1 – LIGHTING THE FIRE

Danielle Randolph sat at her antique secretary desk in her office in her century old Pink Lady Victorian home in Jackson, GA. Her hands were folded and pressed tightly against her lips, fingers interlaced. She stared intently at her reflection in the laptop screen in front of her. Her naturally platinum blonde hair was neatly arranged in the classic bun that she typically wore at the hospital where she had been working as a nurse since college graduation.

She debated about whether to take out the pins that held it in place and let it cascade down her back. Hoonie had always loved her long hair. She wondered if he would be impressed that it was now down past her knees. As appealing as the notion was that playing on the past would give her any type of advantage in dealing with her daughter's biological father, her decades of trained calculating logic from work wove a coldly different reality.

'No,' she thought to herself. The second wealthiest and most powerful Chairman in South Korea would not be swayed by such a blatant attempt at emotional appeals. If anything, it would work against her and not for her. Such a maneuver would diminish her capacity as an adversary in his eyes. Although he would never openly admit it, she knew at the core of her being that he held at least a grudging admiration of her in her ability to keep Angelique's existence hidden from him for almost two decades.

When she had learned that she was pregnant, she dropped out of medical school, legally changed her name, completed nursing school, and moved to a small rural town in the middle of nowhere. She did it all in an effort to protect her daughter from becoming a pawn in the Chairman's corporate chess game. Chaebol machinations outside the legal system were well known to any who even superficially delved into the culture.

Even though she knew that Angelique had dabbled in the realms of KPop and KDrama, she had managed to keep her daughter relatively insulated from that world until the end of her junior year. It was then that a foreign exchange student from Seoul had won her heart. Unfortunately, for everyone concerned, that student was none other than the heir to the first largest, wealthiest, and most powerful family conglomerate.

Things might have settled back to normal once he had returned to South Korea except that the boy had interfered and she had been caught red-handed keeping the scholarship that he had created for her under wraps. Angelique was far too young at the time to understand her reasons for doing what she did nor was her daughter likely to even attempt to do so. She was at that stage where she knew everything.

Danielle knew that she may even have been able to salvage that fiasco but a DNA test, given to her as a graduation present by her best friend in attempt to help her locate her father's family, had revealed the skeleton that she had kept in the closet for so long. The fact that secret was out was at the center of the dilemma that she currently faced.

Once Chairman Min had learned of Angelique's existence, a series of mind games had begun. It was mentally, emotionally, and physically exhausting for everyone close to her daughter. Angelique had aggravated the situation by accepting the proposal of the young man. Unlike America, South Korea still practiced arranged marriages especially at that economic caste. Angelique's engagement had been an unintentional declaration of war between the families.

While Lee Hyung-Joo was ready to sever his family ties if that was what it took for them to be together, Angelique was not so ready to turn her back on the brother that she had just learned that she had. They had quickly developed a strong and loving bond that she did not want to lose.

Angelique had returned to Seoul after breaking her engagement to Lee Hyung-Joo in an attempt to get her father's approval and permission for the wedding. In the end, the only way for her to do that was to blackmail both Chairman Min and Chairman Lee. She had managed that with the help of her fiancé and her best friend, Jessica Yoo. They had threatened to marry each other if Angelique and Hyung-Joo's union was not approved.

The only reason this had worked was that Jessica was a 'nobody.' She had no standing on the social register and a marriage like that would have resulted in Hyung-Joo being disowned and losing his birthright as heir to LH Group. Chairman Lee did not intend to allow three generations of hard work to crumble because his bratty offspring was too blinded by love to realize that almost a quarter million people would lose their jobs if the corporation collapsed. South Korea conglomerates were highly susceptible to scandal based on the morals and behavior of the family members. One such as Hyung-Joo marrying Jessica, even against family wishes, would quickly cause stock prices to plummet. At least Angelique could be legitimized if her DNA records were accepted and verified and Chairman Min had her placed on the family registry.

But Danielle knew Dong-Hoon well enough to know that he would not let the matter rest. He was not about to allow Angelique to live her life in any manner other than what *he* chose. Her job as her mother was to see that didn't happen.

During Angelique's recent visit to Seoul, she had not been idle. She had made plans of her own. All of them depended on the outcome of the video chat that she was about to initiate. Which avenue she decided to travel was up to him. The dread in the pit of her stomach told her that the path was not going to be easy or pleasant.

Danielle's finger hovered hesitantly above the green button on the touch screen that would complete the video call. She took a deep breath and exhaled slowly before making the connection.

***

Chairman Min sat behind his walnut, leather topped executive desk as he waded through the piles of items that demanded his signature. He stiffened when he saw the incoming call. He had no clue as to why that woman would be calling after the havoc that she had created. He briefly entertained the notion of not answering. No, he would hear what she had to say even though he seriously doubted that it could be of any consequence.

"Speak." he commanded.

"Nice to see you again too, Hoonie." Danielle said coldly but smiled reminiscently as she used the affectionate suffix of his given name as she had when they were lovers. She noted that he had aged well despite a few fine lines around his deep brown, almond-shaped eyes. Angelique had inherited quite a few of his features including his eyes. She was never quite able to look at her daughter without also thinking of him. It had only served to strengthen her resolve throughout the years and set plans in motion should this day ever arrive.

"If all you have is small talk, our conversation is at an end." Dong-hoon reached forward to disconnect the call.

"I wouldn't do that if I were you." Danielle warned, a cold edge in her voice.

The Chairman scanned her face for telltale signs of bluffing. He saw none. She met his gaze directly, never breaking eye contact. If anything, the bunched skin beneath her eyes and the crinkles at the side of them indicated that she was laughing at him. He leaned back in his chair.

"You are in no position to make threats." he sneered. He knew all too well her socio-economic status. One call from him, well maybe two, and he could have everything she had ever worked for disappear – home, job, pension. Not to mention that bastard that she had brought into this world. He should have shipped her off to Costa Rica as he had originally planned. He had gotten greedy in thinking that he could arrange an AMMA – Arranged Marriage of Merger and Acquisition – with the Parks two children thereby dethroning the Lee's from the #1 corporate rankings and solidifying their station.

"Nonetheless, I am warning you. Leave her alone and let her live her life as she pleases. You are just being petulant over the fact that she got the best of you." Danielle leaned forward and smirked as she continued, "You should be proud. Your daughter turned out to be just like you."

He refused to acknowledge aloud that he had been stewing over how to crush his illegitimate offspring without backlash on his son, himself or the empire that they had built. Despite the fact that she knew him well enough to figure that out did not change the situation. She was powerless to stop him. So why was she deliberately provoking him?

"I fail to see what you hope to accomplish by spewing vague and idle threats." he harrumphed.

"Don't test me Hoonie. I am telling you for the last time. Leave her alone or you will be sorry." Danielle's jaw was set and determined as she made her final plea. She sat back in her chair and waited.

"Your bravado is amusing but completely ineffectual. Do your best." He fell backward laughing and ended the call.

Danielle Randolph once again folded her hands and pressed them tightly against her lips, fingers interlaced. She stared blankly at the screen in front of her contemplating her choices. She had fervently prayed that it would not come to this but he had left her no other option.

Hoonie simply saw her as a weak, poor, powerless individual. It was a façade that she had cultivated well over the years. She pulled herself upright and squared her shoulders. He should have looked past the superficial.

Chairman Min's anger and focus were completely misplaced. It was *she* who first defied him by disappearing with Angelique in the first place. It was *she* who had sheltered her for nearly two decades from his manipulative mind games. It was *she* who, despite not having the legal title, was just as much a Chairwoman as he was a Chairman. Moreover, whether he believed it yet or not, it would be *she* who bested him last and *she* who would be the one to bring him down. All it would take to set it all in motion would be one phone call.

She eyed the burn phone that had been sitting next to her computer. She briefly wondered whether the events that she was about to set in motion would harm her daughter more than help her. However, it was only a fleeting thought. She knew that her daughter stood absolutely no chance against the combined wealth and power of Chairman Min and Chairman Lee. Not in the long term. Not in the end game. If Angelique were to have any hope of happiness, she could not afford to wait any longer. She needed to set her plan into action now.

Danielle picked up the phone that contained only one other number – another burn phone. She sent a two-word text giving instructions to the recipient. Then she regally stood, closed the lid of her laptop, crossed the room, and threw the phone into the fireplace. She crossed her arms and watched it melt. She should not have to wait long. But it would be agony until then.

***

On the other side of the world, a burn phone vibrated in Choi Yo-Hyun's jacket pocket. His heartbeat quickened. Even though he had waited impatiently for his instructions, he was still startled now that they had arrived. What he was about to do would forever alter many lives, including that of his employer – Min Seung-Hwa.

Yo-Hyun had been with Seung-Hwa as his personal secretary/assistant all through the Young Master's college years and as Seung-Hwa apprenticed to take over the business upon Chairman Min's retirement.

He had come to think of Seung-Hwa as his hyung (older brother). The Young Master allowed him to speak freely on more than one occasion, which normally violated the employer-employee relationship at the corporate level at which he worked. It was during one of these sessions that Yo-Hyun had confessed that he was in love with the Young Master's little sister – Angelique Randolph.

While he knew that nothing would ever come of it because of the difference in their stations, he had been quite clear that he would protect Angelique with his very life if necessary, even over that of Seung-Hwa. He had volunteered to get whatever training was required of him in order to fulfill that promise in the event that the Chairman chose to have Angelique 'disappear' to a remote foreign country as so many other illegitimate Chaebol offspring often had. To his surprise, Seung-Hwa had not fired him on the spot. He took that as a good sign.

Despite that, he was not at all sure that what he was prepared to do would be met with the Young Master's approval even though it was both in his and his sister's best interest. In some ways, he felt like he was betraying him. He only hoped that, should he be caught, he would be given the opportunity to explain himself. And, hopefully forgiven.

Yo-Hyun fished the phone from his pocket and read the short message - IMPLEMENT STAGE-1. Without hesitation, Yo-Hyun sent a mass text and mass email with multiple photo attachments to the group contact that had been created on the phone prior to him being entrusted with it. He systematically deleted everything prior to intentionally dropping the phone into a pitcher of water that was on the conference room table where he had been working. He then retrieved it, wiped it clean of prints with his handkerchief, balled it up inside several pieces of used paper and threw the small bundle into the incinerator chute.

After completing these tasks, he made a mental note to retrieve phone-2 from the floor safe at his apartment when he returned home. Then he went about his normal daily routine as if nothing had happened.

***

Editors of every gossip tabloid regardless of their written or virtual format, received photos of Min Seung-Hwa either carrying or reading a book entitled *Off Seoul Searching* by Angelique Randolph. Each editor questioned how the anonymous sender had managed to secure his or her personal email and personal hand phone number. Each wondered why someone thought those photos were a newsworthy item even if it did involve the 2nd most eligible bachelor in South Korea. Each smelled a story and ordered their staff writers to go with the publication of the photos in the society section with an appropriate sensationalized caption. Each ordered the office secretary to bring them a copy of the book STAT!

EPISODE 2 – WHERE THERE'S SMOKE, THERE'S FIRE

Angelique, Jessica, and Hyung-Joo were gathered around the dining room table in the Athens, GA apartment that the girls called home. It was typical student housing near the university meaning that it was small with austere white walls, and lacked many of the amenities that most people prefer. But the lack of a dishwasher did not stop the two females who had been best friends since the first day of middle school from turning it into a warm and cozy abode.

Angelique was quite skilled at crafts and traces of her handiwork could be found everywhere. She had made macramé plant hangers for Jessica's plants that hung in every window. Jessica took care of the plants because Angelique had a brown thumb rather than a green one and could somehow manage to kill even air ferns. A crocheted afghan in the school colors of red, white, and black somehow managed not to clash with the forest green microfiber sectional that separated the dining room from the living room. The placemats and center mat at the small square table were quilted and served to keep the heat from plates as well as condensation from cold drinks from damaging the furniture finish. The girls knew that even inexpensive things could last a long time if they received proper care.

Hyung-Joo wondered how he had ever thought this place sparse and lowly. He had been raised with a silver spoon in his mouth yet somehow had always known and felt that how he lived was nothing more than a prison cell albeit a luxurious one. Nevertheless, at first he could not help but make comparisons to what he wanted for Angelique and what he could have afforded to give her to what she actually had.

Eventually he came to see how all those little facets of her personality woven together with the energy and love she put into her crafts created something that could not be bought in any store at any price. This was the woman to whom he had given his heart and this was the way he wanted to share his life with her.

She had gotten a taste this past semester of how quickly wealth and power could complicate and ruin a person's life. He hoped that she would now understand why he wanted her to stop worrying about him being disinherited and instead focus on what would make them happy together as a couple instead of as individuals. Because of school, it would still be a year before they had to choose which country would be there ultimate home.

He still caught glimpses of how her recent experiences haunted her in the sadness that often crept into her eyes even though a smile played on her lips and laughter spilled from her mouth. He knew that thoughts of her brother's happiness were never far from her mind. He also knew that she fretted about whether or not Seung-Hwa would have the courage to stand his ground with their father and insist on marrying the girl that he loved rather than one that was chosen for him.

The fact that her best friend was that girl added to her burden as she somehow also felt responsible for both of them since she was the one who had brought them together in the first place. Perhaps it was too soon to have expected her to let go of all of those concerns. It had only been a little less than a week since their return from Seoul.

However, that was also precisely why he was currently sitting with them at their dining room table in Athens, GA instead of being back at his place in Cambridge, MA. Before he flew back to start the semester, they had to iron out school schedules – his from Harvard and the girls from UGA - and pick a wedding date. They had gotten his father's word to announce the engagement within a week with summer nuptials. They needed to decide soon.

School calendars had been printed and placed on either side of the weekly planner that Angelique preferred to use. Above the three of those was an actual wedding planner that broke down what tasks had to be done by when. While Hyung-Joo would have previously simply delegated those tasks to someone else, he now was faced with a marriage of love and choice rather than one that was arranged by his parents and dictated to him.

He understood completely why the two girls wanted to do all of it themselves and was all too happy to be part of the decision making process. For the first time in a long time, he watched them huddled together as they had always done through high school while they poured over all the material and tried to figure out when they were going to manage to accomplish everything around their college course load. The sight warmed his heart and he felt as if it would melt.

Angelique looked up to catch him studying her. She drowned in his deep brown eyes and smiled at the tousled mop that he called hair. He would tame it with salon products when he went anywhere outside, but this was how she thought of him whenever they were apart. How had she ever been lucky enough to attract her own honest to goodness real life flower boy?

"It looks like our spring breaks are different weeks. When ours ends, yours begins. That is going to make it really tough. Will you be okay with video conferencing?"

He was about to remind her that money was not an issue and that, as long as she made any appointments for Friday nights or during the weekends, he could fly back every weekend if that was what she wanted. He was also going to remind her that his Black American Express Centurion card would guarantee that any business anywhere would make appointments for any time her little heart desired. Her phone rang before he got the chance.

Angelique jumped to her feet at whatever comment had been made from the other end. Then she started to shriek at the top of her lungs. Neither Hyung-Joo nor Jessica knew whether or not to be alarmed. Angelique tended to over-react to everything. It was what had earned her the nickname of 'drama queen' since kindergarten. Angelique herself had added the 'K' to the front during her freshman year of high school when she had first discovered KPop and

KDrama. She wore the title like a badge of honor. None of it was an act. It was simply a part of who she was.

Angelique ran out of breath and stopped screaming long enough to draw in a deep lung full of fresh oxygen. She managed to end the conversation confirming that she had gotten it all and would look for all the details in the email that would be sent shortly.

Hyung-Joo and Jessica waited expectantly. Hyung-Joo quickly noted that Angelique's eyes sparkled. There was no trace of any of the torment that he had seen ever present since their return from South Korea. It always amazed him how quickly she could shift from one extreme to another. Despite that fact, he was fairly certain that whatever had managed to wipe away any lingering pain must be pretty spectacular.

"You are neee-verrr going to guess what just happened." The tone in her voice dared them to guess.

"No clue. Are you going to tell us or are you going to make us wait all night?" Jessica prompted her friend to elaborate.

"I can't believe it myself. I have to pinch myself to make sure that I'm awake. OUCH!"

Jessica rolled her eyes. Hyung-Joo laughed.

"Are you ready for this?" she leaned forward, placing both hands on the table.

They nodded to assure her that they were. Playing along and being Angelique's captive audience was now their current role.

"That," she pointed to the cell phone on the table, "was my literary agent. Foreign sales of my book have exploded. And, get this, they were approached by an independent cable network about turning it into a KDrama! And, on top of all that, they want me to join the writing staff!"

She let out another shriek and started jumping up and down. She was so wrapped up in her own world that she didn't realize that neither Jessica nor Hyung-Joo seemed to share her exuberance.

In fact, both Hyung-Joo and Jessica were staring at each other. Their eyes were wide. Their mouths hung open. They were beyond flabbergasted. They were in shock. It was clear to them that Angelique did not see what this portended.

Angelique had written the book after her return from her first trip to Seoul as therapy. She used her writing as a method to work through all her emotions that warred within her after discovering her true family lineage. She also had to deal with the unveiled truth that Hyung-Joo was also Chaebol and not just any run-of-the-mill foreign exchange student as he had pretended to be.

Though couched as fiction since many scenes had been dramatized, it was primarily an autobiography. Anyone that knew her could easily identify all the players in the script. She had originally published it on Wattpad as she wrote each chapter. Since she already had a decent size fan base from her fanfic writing, it had gotten quite a bit of attention rather quickly. That, in turn, caught the attention of a small publishing house. It was the publishing company's policy to only deal with authors who had agents, so Angelique had gotten one. Most first time authors had trouble finding an agent, but it was easier since she already had a guaranteed contract.

Angelique finally realized that she was the only one celebrating.

"Aren't you happy for me?" she wanted to know, face still glowing.

Jessica did a facepalm.

"Aish ..." Hyung-Joo closed his eyes, ran his fingers through his hair, and let the curse hang in the air as he hung his head in his hands.

He looked up at her and asked her solemnly, "Just how many times do you think that you can get away with antagonizing our fathers before they retaliate in a manner that you are definitely going to wish they hadn't?"

"I don't understand what you mean." Angelique's face became more sober, a furrow appearing between her eyes.

Hyung-Joo sighed softly. Angelique was far from stupid. She was actually very intelligent. However, she was also very naïve. This often made her quite clueless at times, this being one of them.

"Do you have any idea what the words 'low profile' mean?" he asked shaking his head in disbelief. "How many times have you promised it and how many times have you broken it?

"It was one thing when your book was only reaching a couple hundred thousand people in an American market. There is slim to no threat level since no one here cares who you are and single parents are common. It is quite another story altogether to broadcast your identity to fifty million people in the country where you have yet to be placed on the family register and where illegitimate offspring and their parents are ostracized. You've just taken us – you and me - from DEFCON 5 to DEFCON 1 in one phone call."

Hyung-Joo spoke sternly as if he were a parent speaking to a child. But sometimes with Angelique, that was the only way to get across the magnitude of a situation.

"Oh, that." Angelique dismissed it with a wave of her hand and was right back on Cloud 9. "There are a gazillion KDramas with the same basic rag-to-riches and hidden children themes. This will be just one more and no one will be any the wiser." She continued to dance her little jig.

"C'mon … be happy for me." She pranced around and pulled at his sleeves.

"My book is going to be a KDrama! I mean, it was always a secret wish way deep down but I never really dared to hope. Do you have any idea what that can mean for my career as a writer?" She let out another squeal.

Just then, Hyung-Joo's phone played the music that he had assigned as Seung-Hwa's ringtone. He turned it around so that she could see who was calling.

"You see who it is? Your brother. President of my anti-fan club. Or have you forgotten how many times he's threatened to kill me? I haven't. Three!"

Hyung-Joo was jogging her memory from the previous summer when she had learned his true identity and that he was engaged to another – the AMMA that his father had set. She had been in a state of shock from the discovery and had stumbled off the sidewalk and into traffic. Seung-Hwa had made it clear that he held Hyung-Joo responsible for Angelique's accident and subsequent coma.

Seung-Hwa had started to come around but they were far from the bromance that they had shared in elementary school. Chairman Min had poisoned Seung-Hwa against him once the boy had entered middle school as his father had begun to groom him for his eventual take-over of the family's corporate holdings.

"Are you getting even the slightest inkling of the seriousness of this yet?" Hyung-Joo asked as he jabbed his finger on the answer call button and then harder still on the two that read 'speaker' and 'extra volume.'

"Yeoboseyo," he greeted the caller informally. Though he didn't intend for it to happen, his irritation at Angelique came across in his voice.

"Just what in the hell did you two think that you were going to accomplish with this stunt?" Seung-Hwa demanded to know. The inflection in his voice made it clear that he wanted the answer yesterday.

Hearing the disapproval in the voices of the two most important men in her life, Angelique was having a change of heart. She still did not really see why it was such a big deal, but her fiancé and brother seemed to feel that it was so she was rapidly becoming anxious.

"O-ppa," she drug out the word as she wailed.

It was unclear to whom she was speaking since the term could have been used for either a boyfriend or older brother. Maybe she was being deliberately ambiguous. They both supposed that it really didn't much matter.

"Please don't be mad at me. I didn't do anything wrong. I swear." Angelique turned on the water works and tears streamed in rivulets down her cheeks and rolled off her chin, creating large 'plops' on the quilted placemat.

Hyung-Joo caught himself. It was totally unfair to Angelique to view it that way. Angelique truly felt and experienced things in extreme ways and it was easy enough to think that it was intentional. He was exasperated at the situation but that was no reason to take it out on her. He rubbed his temples where a stress headache was beginning to form.

They slowly and methodically pieced together what they knew which really amounted to very little.

Someone had released photos of Seung-Hwa with Angelique's book to all the editor's in town. He had decided to read it because both Hyung-Joo and Angelique had fairly recently asked him if he had done so. The implication in both incidents was that he would understand the situation more if he had read it. He decided that he really should read it for himself and that it might be a good way to get to know his sister better.

The photos that were sent out were not of good quality so it was unlikely to be a professional hired by any sort of rival – business or personal. They were taken in public places such as on his way to the car or at a coffee shop so highly unlikely that they would be able to find the photographer. They had considered searching the CCTV footage in the areas, but there was no way to pinpoint exact dates and times as these were daily stops and routines.

Chairman Min had gotten wind of it first when a few editors had called the main office asking for a comment. It was well known that the Min family was not one that you wanted to provoke. His personal secretary had informed him immediately, correctly gauging the situation and pulling him from a luncheon meeting.

Chairman Min had gone into immediate action and had the photos pulled from as many publications as possible by resorting to threats, favors, bribes, or any combination of the three. As a result, only a handful had actually been published, but it was enough.

Seoul netizens tended to be curious about the minutest details involving anyone with even a hint of celebrity status. This fact alone was a key driving force in the Korean entertainment industry. While technically the sites used for the downloading of Angelique's books would not work directly in South Korea, there were US forwarding services that many Koreans used both for shipping of actual physical goods as well as virtual merchandise.

Because of all these factors, it took only a few hours for the photos and Angelique's book to go viral. Her book was currently trending at #5 for most searches and rising.

Jessica asked if it were okay for her to add something. Angelique looked at her as if to say, 'why is that even something you need to ask?' Hyung-Joo; however, knew why she did it. He gave her a wink and a 'thumbs up' sign to signify that she had done well.

Angelique raised an eyebrow quizzically and Hyung-Joo mouthed the word 'later.' She pursed her lips indicating that she wasn't happy about it but that she would temporarily accept it as an answer.

Korea was still very much a patriarchal society. While that was slowly changing in the larger cities and among the middle and lower classes, that was not the case in the upper class circles that they traveled or in rural areas.

It would not have been socially acceptable for the girls to interrupt the men talking even though both males knew that the girls were hearing them. Angelique actually knew this and had acted accordingly on many occasions. It just appeared that she had forgotten that it applied to this one.

More likely, knowing Angelique, she probably felt that since it involved him and her brother it didn't count. While Hyung-Joo would have chosen to ignore it, he knew without a doubt that Seung-Hwa would not. They were 180 degrees apart on this point.

"I think that it's highly suspicious that this falls at this particular time." Jessica elaborated when prompted by Seung-Hwa.

"We were just looking at the calendar and discussing wedding dates for the engagement announcement when you called. What if this is an attempt by Chairman Lee to delay the wedding?"

The sharp intake of breath from both males indicated two things to her. One was that neither of them had thought about that possibility. The second was that she could very well have hit the nail on the head.

"Why would it delay the wedding?" Angelique wanted to know.

Seung-Hwa and Hyung-Joo both had first hand knowledge of the answer to that question since both families had broadcasting, filming, and entertainment companies in their holdings portfolio.

They patiently explained to her that the filming of one of her beloved KDramas was very different than filming a typical US TV show. Casting alone could take several months with writers being actively involved in the decision making process. There would then be several months of rehearsals both acting and vocal for the musical soundtrack. This drama would also require English coaching since half the story took place in America. This would extend the pre-production time. Only two or three episodes would be filmed ahead of time and the remaining episodes would be shot while the others were airing. This would result in very long workdays, often as many as 18 hours per day. An average 24 episode KDrama airing twice per week would take at least 8 months and probably closer to a year to produce.

Hyung-Joo asked if it were possible to pull the drama. Seung-Hwa let him know that it had been picked up by an independent cable company and not anything that either family could control.

As the reality of it began to set in, Angelique began to cry. First at the thought of not getting married in a few months and then at not having her drama made. Deep, heart-wrenching sobs escaped from her throat. Jessica got up and wrapped her arms around her dearest friend to comfort her.

"In other words, I have to choose between my dream and my love. Either way I lose a piece of my heart and my soul." If it were possible, her wails got louder.

Hyung-Joo got up and went to her. Jessica stepped back out of the way and he gathered her up in his arms. They had been through much worse than this. He held her close with one hand on her back and the other on the back of her head. He rested his chin on top of her head as he soothed her.

"Shhhh. Gwenchana. You don't have to choose. I won't make you choose. There isn't anything that's going to happen in the next year that will ever change how I feel about you. You aren't going to lose me."

He put a finger under her chin and tilted her face upward. He lowered his face to hers and lightly touched his lips to hers. They were salty from her tears.

"I can't go with you though. I can't leave now that the semester has started. I have a M-Tu-W schedule so I can make it out for long weekends here and there but it's going to depend on my project due dates."

He turned his face toward the phone in the center of the table and spoke a little louder.

"Did you catch that hyung? Promise to take care of her for me." Hyung-Joo thought that sending her to Seung-Hwa for protection was getting to be a habit. A habit that he really would have preferred not to rely upon.

"Yaksokha. Keokjangma."

Hyung-Joo trusted Seung-Hwa to keep his promise. However, he would worry nonetheless.

EPISODE 3 – ADDING FUEL TO THE FIRE

Angelique Randolph stepped off the plane at Incheon Airport in the early evening hours. She was tired and in pain.

She was never able to sleep well on a plane since she preferred to sleep on her stomach. This was impossible to do in coach class, which is the ticket type that was reserved for her by the network producing the drama. She may not have slept at all even if she had been able to get into her preferred position considering that her ears were killing her.

She had always had trouble equalizing the pressure in her ears when she flew. They just refused to cooperate and would not pop. In the past, she had tried all the methods that were suggested and the only one that seemed to work was to turn herself upside down and allow the Eustachian tubes to drain. Sixteen hours of flight time in pain would keep anyone awake. She needed to find a family rest room in order to have the privacy she needed to put herself into such an awkward position.

She was so focused on locating the nearest rest room that would suit her purpose that she was caught completely by surprise when someone placed their hand under her elbow and began to steer her off in the opposite direction that she had intended to go.

"Ajussi Ryu!" She greeted enthusiastically when she glanced sideways and realized that it was one of the two bodyguards that had been assigned to her during her last visit. During that trip she had arrived without luggage so he had lent her his parka so that she could go outside and play in the snow. She went to throw her arms around his neck to give him a hug, but he stepped backward out of reach.

"Pabo!" she slapped her forehead with the heel of her palm. Public displays of affection are not acceptable in South Korea. She did a 45 degree bow in his direction instead. It was then that she saw another pair of legs approach to stand beside him.

If there was one thing that Angelique knew better than KDrama, it was clothes. Of course, she knew about them from watching KDramas where sponsorship and product placement drove the fashion industry. The navy blue and azure pinstripe Gucci wool slacks neatly cuffed a pair of Salvatore Ferragamo black leather oxfords. Judging from the stiff stance, they could only belong to one person – her father.

Her brother had told her and Hyung-Joo that he would meet her. Why had he sent their father instead? She stayed doubled over and greeted him in English since he disliked hearing his native language in her Southern drawl.

When she stood back upright, her father was in front of her and she was flanked on either side by black suits. Despite the fact that they had been very kind to her when she had been in their charge, their posture left no doubt that they were Chairman Min's men. There would be no appealing to them for help. They would do with her whatever he ordered them to do.

They stood for several moments just staring at each other. It seemed like an eternity. Angelique's mind was racing for an explanation and a plan. Her father broke the silence first.

"You will follow me." he commanded as he turned on his heels.

"But I was supposed to meet Seung-Hwa for dinner." she planted her feet firmly and refused to move.

Her father gave no indication that he had heard her and never faltered in his steps and kept a slow and steady stride away from her. The bodyguards each took an arm and urged her forward taking only a split second to open their jacket to show that they were armed with weapons and hypodermics.

Angelique knew there was no sense in making a scene. Considering how her body had responded to a low dose pain-killer when she had sprained her ankle last summer, she had no doubt that whatever was in those syringes would drop her like a horse.

She also thought she had a pretty good idea of where they were going. She cursed herself for not telling Seung-Hwa about their father's threat to exile her if she did not agree to an AMMA with Park Ji-Tae, Seung-Hwa's 'bad boy' friend. However, she had not thought that he would believe her. She still didn't think that he would.

Seung-Hwa knew that their father struggled with her existence but truly believed that he would eventually come around. She did not blame him for sticking up for him. Blood is blood.

Angelique's heart leapt into her throat as she caught sight of her brother and his secretary. Her excitement was short lived; however, as her father maneuvered himself so that he stood in front of her blocking her sight line to him. Even though Seung-Hwa was over six feet tall, she was only 5'2" and her father was too close for her to make visual contact.

This also meant that she was unable to use any of the secret non-verbal cues that they had developed between them. She didn't know if her father actually knew about them or if it was just her bad luck. Either way, there was no way for her to signal him so that Seung-Hwa would know how distressed she was or that she was in serious trouble.

She wouldn't even be able to give him any verbal cues either as the guards were standing ready with their needles. One false move on her part would send her to la-la land. Since she had a history of fainting under stress, it would look as if the excitement and travel had taken their toll.

Seung-Hwa was caught in his own difficult dilemma. He was unable to maneuver to a spot that allowed him visual access to his sister. In addition, he had no reason that would appear legitimate to demand that it be given to him. He bowed to his father and decided to play it safe.

"Abeoji. I didn't know that you were coming. I could have saved myself a trip. But, since you are here, would you like to join us for dinner?"

Seung-Hwa knew that he was walking a very fine line. He would have to tread very carefully.

"I have things to discuss with … your sister." Chairman Min cleared his throat. He still struggled to use that relationship term as if it were natural. Moreover, he absolutely, positively refused to refer to the little bastard as his daughter. "In private," he added.

"Certainly. I understand." he acknowledged. Then he talked past his father to Angelique, "Did you have a good flight?"

To Angelique, it seemed that the guards moved in closer.

"Yes, oppa." Angelique tried to put as much warmth into the reply as possible. While she was tired and in pain, being drugged was not how she wanted to go to sleep.

Seung-Hwa wasn't sure what else he could do under the circumstances. He was sure that Angelique was going to get an earful from their father. He had to listen to it for days. He would have liked to have been present to mediate but Father's tone had made it crystal clear that his presence was unwelcome. "Give me a call later tonight," he told her as he turned to leave.

Angelique knew that there was no way in hell her father was going to let her call him but she answered him anyway. "Will do." And hiccupped.

Seung-Hwa stopped and looked back over his shoulder. "Are you okay?"

"I'm fine." She hiccupped again. "I just need some water." And yet again. The guards eyed her suspiciously. She held her breath to try and get rid of them.

"Alright then. Bye for now." he waved even though he knew she couldn't see him.

On his way back to the garage, he took out his hand phone and dialed Hyung-Joo. He had promised to call him. "Angelique arrived safely," he informed him.

"Good. Let me talk to her for a minute."

"You'll have to call her directly. She's not here at the moment."

"What do you mean she's not there? Where is she?" Panic started to rise in Hyung-Joo's voice as a feeling of dread crept up his spine. He shivered in fear.

"She's with father. He picked her up. He said that he had things to discuss with her."

"And you let him?" Hyung-Joo held the phone away from his ear and stared at the screen in disbelief.

"Exactly what is it that I was supposed to do? He's going to read her the riot act and he made a point of telling me that my presence wasn't required. She's going to call me tonight."

Hyung-Joo breathed out a sigh of relief. "So she's okay?"

"Except for a case of the hiccups, yeah, she's fine," he assured him.

Hyung-Joo went cold as all the blood drained from his body. He reached out a hand and steadied himself against the wall.

Angelique had a habit of living the KDramas that she had watched. In one, *Pinocchio*, the female lead had a disorder of the autonomic nervous system known as Pinocchio Syndrome. This disorder caused her to hiccup whenever she told a lie. The bigger the lie, the worse the hiccups. Angelique had used it with both him and Jessica in the past as a secret code.

However, even though the disorder was fictitious, Angelique being the KDrama Queen that she was had internalized it to the point where she actually manifested the same symptoms. It was very difficult, if not impossible, for her to tell a deliberate lie.

He choked down his apprehension and spoke calmly yet purposefully, "Listen to me very carefully. There is no time for questions and no time to waste. I will explain in detail later. Right now you need to understand that was a code and she is in danger. You have to find her. Now!"

Seung-Hwa took off at a mad run with his secretary at his heels.

***

Danielle Randolph, sat at the kitchen table with her morning coffee. Both hands were wrapped around the mug as she raised it to her lips to sip.

She contemplated the bank of cloned phones and recording equipment that were in front of her. She took a minute to replay the message. She picked up the burn phone and sent a two-word text to the only number in the contact list.

***

Choi Yo-Hyun felt the burner phone that had replaced the last one vibrate in his pocket. There were only two possible messages – initiate or abort. Considering what was currently transpiring, he was fairly certain which text he would be reading but he had to verify.

Earlier in the day he had used his instructions from burner phone-2 to post a cryptic message on a group page that would either now be activated or immobilized. A VPN and Proxy server would fake the IP address and would make it extremely difficult to trace.

Not being able to receive reply comments would not be a concern for the purpose intended.

He took a moment to duck behind an advertising display. He opened and read the text. INITIATE STAGE-3. Yo-Hyun sent the pre-programmed message to the forum section of the group's bulletin board.

Yo-Hyun wiped his prints from the hand phone with his handkerchief, took out some paper napkins from his pocket to wrap it in, sealed it in the quart size Ziploc baggie in which it had been given to him, and dashed to catch up to his employer. He dropped the bundle in the first trash receptacle that he passed.

***

Seung-Hwa had stopped and was trying to determine which way to turn. He knew the direction in which they had been headed but he now stood at an intersection. He methodically scanned each possibility hoping that he would see them. His attempt was fruitless. Incheon was one of the largest airports in the world. A wrong turn at any junction would be disastrous.

He felt a hand on his shoulder and turned to see his secretary looking worried and pensive. Seung-Hwa put his hand on Yo-Hyun's shoulder in return.

"I know your feelings for her even though you don't speak them. We will find her," he assured the man who had been by his side for over half a decade.

"I think I know where they may be," Yo-Hyun said as he opened the photo gallery on his personal hand phone. "I remembered Angelique's insistence that she felt that Chairman Min was going to have her vanish without a trace. When you told me that she was coming back to Seoul, I went snooping in your father's desk. Jwesong hamnida."

Yo-Hyun cringed and apologized for what could be taken as an act of betrayal and mean his immediate dismissal at best; his own disappearance at worst. Certainly it would have been to the Chairman. He hoped that Danielle Randolph's insistence that would not be the case with Seung-Hwa was correct.

Yo-Hyung scrolled through his pictures for the one that he needed. It was important that it was buried and did not seem too readily available. Having it right at the top may have looked suspicious. He found the one that he was looking for and handed the Galaxy S20 Ultra 5G over to his employer.

Seung-Hwa pinched his fingers in the center and expanded them so that he could more easily read the document in the photo. It was a page from a report that detailed the family's foreign holdings. One of their Costa Rica locations was circled with an asterisk beside it. In his father's handwriting was the name and number of one of their private pilots.

"I'm sorry that I didn't bring it to you sooner. I wasn't sure that it actually meant anything but under the circumstances …." he left the sentence hang, unfinished.

A lump formed in Seung-Hwa's throat as he fought a private battle with his emotions. He had not thought his father capable of such an act. The Chairman was well aware of how dearly he loved his sister even if the relationship was not officially acknowledged. He couldn't believe that his own father would do this to him. It was why he continually argued with Angelique against what he thought was a completely preposterous idea.

He cleared his throat and swallowed hard. At least now he knew which way they were headed. "Good man," he complimented as he turned and ran down the hallway toward the exit that would eventually lead to where the private aircraft were hangered.

Yo-Hyun ran to keep pace.

***

Angelique stepped out of the terminal building and onto the tarmac with her two bodyguards. Her father had bidden her a not-so-fond farewell inside the terminal. She brought her arm up to cover her eyes as flashes began to go off. Her escorts managed a surreptitious and hasty retreat.

Behind a cordon, were hundreds of sasaeng. Though despised by most for their obsessive, near stalking behavior towards anyone in the entertainment industry, Angelique welcomed their invasion of her privacy under the circumstances.

Being permitted past the barrier and onto the tarmac were Seung-Hwa and Yo-Hyun. She was never so glad to see her brother in her life but she had to refrain from rushing forward and throwing herself into his arms.

As he approached, she gave him a 90-degree bow and he returned it with a 15-degree one indicative of his status. At the same time, he reached out, took her hand, and shook it.

Angelique was thankful for the gesture. She desperately needed human contact to stop shaking. He used the customary American greeting as a chance to squeeze her hand to let her know that it was going to be okay. She returned the squeeze with a grateful smile.

Yo-Hyun reached into his portfolio and pulled forth a copy of her book, which he handed to her brother.

Angelique's smile and eyes grew larger. She brought her hands up to cover her heart and said, "Awww," as Seung-Hwa opened it to the first page and held it out to her along with a pen. In perfect, accent-free English he asked, "Sign, please?"

The sasaeng cheered wildly. The camera flashes went crazy. Within minutes, *Off Seoul Searching* by Angelique Randolph climbed to #2 on trending searches as the photos and videos taken by the crowd were uploaded to the internet. It was only a matter of hours before it would reach #1. There was no way that she could 'disappear' now.

***

Halfway around the world Danielle Randolph smiled to herself as she drained the last of her coffee from her mug. She opened her laptop and got back to work.

EPISODE 4 – OUT OF THE FRYING PAN, INTO THE FIRE

It took hours for the crowd to dissipate. It seemed that for every autograph she signed, every selca she took, or every high touch she gave, ten more took their place. Eventually though the crowd thinned.

She willingly and gratefully allowed Yo-Hyun to usher her toward the waiting car with his right hand on her back. The chauffeur opened the door and she managed to hold her composure until it was closed. Once hidden from the world behind the heavily tinted glass, Angelique's composure disintegrated.

She leaned forward and buried her head in her hands. Deep sobs wracked her tiny frame. Her body shook violently and her teeth chattered.

Seung-Hwa knew from two previous experiences that these were symptoms of hormone fluctuations from her recent trauma. She had been riding high on adrenaline for hours and now her system was crashing.

He shrugged out of his coat and asked his secretary to do the same. He bundled the coats around her to keep her warm and had her lean back into him for additional warmth and comfort. Gradually her breathing slowed to normal and the shivering subsided.

"Komowo," she said without lifting her head. She didn't even have the energy to do that. She was extremely tired and weak. The combination of the flight and her experience was taking its toll on her body.

"I can't take full credit for any of that. Yo-Hyun figured out the location. The mob was your guardian angel flying overtime. I just played the hand that was dealt to me and used the crowd and its capabilities to your advantage."

"Still, komowo."

Seung-Hwa squeezed her tighter. Angelique lay there gathering warmth and strength from her brother. She watched the Seoul scenery go by outside the window. Her eyelids were growing heavy with the motion of the vehicle. She was very near to sleep when she caught sight of a landmark that alarmed her and she sat bolt upright.

"Where are we going?" she asked in a shaky voice bordering on hysteria.

"Home," he tried to continue but Angelique cut him off and shook him off.

"You have to be kidding me. Let me out! Now!" she lunged for the door handle.

Seung-Hwa wrapped both his arms around her and pulled her back into him. She struggled against his large, muscular body. Seung-Hwa let her wear herself out while gently whispering 'gwenchana' in her ear. Since she was already exhausted, it did not take long for her to cease her struggles. As she went limp in his arms, she began to whimper softly. He hugged her as tightly as he could.

"I know that you don't think so, but at the moment it really is the safest place for you to be. It will take time for me to put together my own team of bodyguards for you. Ones that answer to me and not to Father. Until then, it's best to have you nearby where I can keep an eye on you.

"In addition, you are, at least for now, a full-blown celebrity. That will eventually die down, but we will take advantage of the time it will buy us. Father is not stupid. He knows that he will need to wait for his next opportunity. To make a move now would turn you into a martyr. That's the last thing that he wants. Mianhaeyo, yeodongsaeng for not believing you. I will be extra vigilant from now on so there is no next time.

"You will need to be at the studio starting Monday. I will work on making sure that the security is beefed up there as well. I will worry about location shoots once I have an actual shooting schedule and I know where and when they will be filmed. In addition, I will look into getting you an apartment closer to your work.

"But all of this can't be done tonight. So you will have to be patient for a few days while I get all the chickens lined up in a row."

Angelique chuckled softly. She didn't have the energy for anything more than that. Her brother spoke excellent English. So much so that it was easy to forget that he wasn't a native speaker. But there were times where it was very obvious.

"Ducks, brother dear. Ducks. Get all your *ducks* in a row," she quietly corrected his idiom. It was the last thing she remembered before falling into a deep and dreamless slumber.

***

Angelique rolled onto her back. She put her arms out and stretched, yawning loudly. She balled her fingers into little fists and rubbed the sleep from her eyes. Her eyelids fluttered open and then closed as her body debated with her mind as to whether or not she should get up or roll back over for more sleep. She snuggled down into the luxurious covers appreciating their softness and warmth. She felt like she was floating, the mattress and bedding conforming to her body. She left her eyes closed as she played with the silk fabric, rolling it back and forth between her fingers.

She smiled a sleepy little smile as awareness began to seep into her consciousness. She was in her room. Her brother must have carried her in from the car.
She took a deep breath and smelled the roses that she knew her brother had arranged to be placed there. It was their favorite flower. One of the many little things that they had in common.

She opened her eyes and surveyed her surroundings. The one room was as large as her entire apartment back in Georgia. The ivory white headboard and footboard featured a hand carved scallop shell in the center of each. There was a matching armoire, nightstand, vanity, and desk. The silk down comforter and pillow shams were solid pink; the lace edging on each had tiny, delicate, hand-embroidered pink rosebuds. A pale pink ball made of capiz shells carved into rosette shapes, hung from the center of the room and gave the area a soft, warm, glow. Sheer, pink lace curtains hung at the windows and double glass door that led to a balcony.

The room was every girl's fantasy. She was no exception. She had known when she left that she was going to miss it. She had never expected to see it again. She heard the latch on the door click and sat up, fluffing the pillows behind her. She knew before it opened that it would be Kang Yoon-Suk, the personal maid that had been assigned to her during her last visit. She knew that Seung-Hwa would keep his promise and that it would be a very short list of those who would be allowed to interact with her.

Yoon-Suk was the daughter of two of the other employees. Her mother was one of the team of chefs that served world class dining at the estate. Her father was the Chairman's chauffer. The two girls weren't that far apart in age and Angelique had befriended the girl despite her brother's warnings that it was both dangerous and inappropriate to be chummy with the staff.

Angelique was wise enough to know that she couldn't share her deepest secret with her and, like the majority of the staff, Yoon-Suk believed her to be a very distant cousin from America. But since Angelique had no other friends in Korea, Yoon-Suk was a pleasant companion to share idle idol gossip and with whom she could watch KDramas.

Yoon-Suk carried a tray with a coffee service and fresh hotteok - a deep-fried, sweet pancake filled with hot, cinnamon flavored syrup and topped with chopped walnuts. It was one of her comfort foods and she was glad to have it this morning after her ordeal the previous evening.

"The Young Master said that you would be wanting this." Yoon-Suk's voice held a note of disbelief since Angelique often skipped food until at least her second cup of coffee.

"The Young Master was right!" Angelique exclaimed as she pulled her legs under her making plenty of room for the breakfast tray on the king sized bed, "At least this time!" Both girls giggled. Angelique patted the top of the covers indicating that the girl should sit and join her.

Yoon-Suk smiled but shook her head as she set down the tray. "The Young Master says that you have only an hour to get ready before you have to leave to run some errands with him so you can be ready for work tomorrow. Are you really going to be working on a KDrama?"

Angelique felt like she was hearing it for the first time. No matter how many times she thought of it, it still felt the same. She grinned from ear-to-ear and nodded repeatedly looking like a bobble-head doll.

"I have a pre-production meeting with the producers early tomorrow to get the casting interview schedule which will probably run all day," Angelique informed her with wide eyes.

Yoon-Suk was now mesmerized and completely drawn in. "Who will you cast for the male lead? I think Kang Daniel would be perfect! He has those same adorable dimples that you describe for Song Chi-won."

Angelique threw back the covers and got out of bed, sliding her feet into her slippers which Seung-Hwa must have set out the night before. She grabbed the girl and hugged her.

"Oh, don't I wish! But this is a small independent cable company without the resources available to the likes of SBS and

KBS," she named the two networks with the largest market shares of KDramas, "so it will be debuts for most, if not all, of the cast. Help me pick out something to wear." Angelique took the girl by the hand and drug her to one of the two doors in the room.

The walk-in closet doubled as a changing room. It was lined with built in shelves and racks of various sizes. There was a section for shoes, handbags, accessories, as well as areas for hanging different lengths of clothing. There were drawers that pulled out specifically designed for holding jewelry.

Every space was filled during her last trip thanks to her brother who had spent an outrageous amount of money to make sure that she was dressed properly as befitted her station. She had chosen to leave it all behind when she left. She was glad to note that her father hadn't burned everything out of spite.

She put together a complete Dolce & Gabbana ensemble of winter white – pants, turtleneck, and jacket. Then she completed the outfit with deep butterscotch Louis Vuitton scarf, beret, and handbag. Her boots also bore the LV logo but matched the color of her pantsuit.

Angelique held them up against herself in the full-length mirror that was centered on the back wall. The outfit was both stylish and professional. She had no idea where she and her brother were going, but she should be covered for anything short of clubbing. Since it was way too early in the day for that and definitely not Seung-Hwa's style, she decided that she was safe. In addition, the colors would highlight her eyes, hair, and skin tone. She had Yoon-Suk lay them out on the bed while she quickly jumped into the shower.

The other door in the room led to the bathroom. It was just as feminine as the bedroom with swirled pink and white marble throughout. In the center of the room was a free-standing island with a sunken bubble tub inset big enough to be considered a small swimming pool. During her previous visit, she had loved lounging in that tub while watching her KDramas. But she didn't have time for a luxurious bubble bath this morning.

She crossed the room to the walk-in shower that was large enough for an entire family. There were multiple rain showerheads above and a series of spray nozzles in multiple rows along the walls. She thought of it as the human equivalent of a car wash. She quickly showered and wrapped herself in a rose-colored bath sheet to do her make-up.

After Yoon-Suk had helped her dress, she sent a text to her brother telling him that she would meet him at the car. As an afterthought, she grabbed another hotteok from the tray, and stuffed it in her mouth. Then she took the back stairs used by the staff so that she did not run the risk of bumping into her father. It did not escape her notice that her brother's personal secretary was following her at a discrete distance.

EPISODE 5 – IRONS IN THE FIRE

Angelique sat beside her brother in the backseat of the Mercedes Sedan. Choi Yo-Hyun was driving. Angelique noticed that the privacy partition was open. It said much about his relationship with his 'employee'. Her brother trusted very few people.

She waited for him to be ready to talk. While most people wouldn't have recognized it, she had learned to see past his stoic façade. There were little nuances that weren't obvious to most because he never let anyone close enough to discover them. For one, his dark brown wave hung over his eye rather than being swept back into place. This told her that his eyes, while looking forward and taking in the scenery, were in reality turned inward working out something that he didn't dare yet vocalize or commit to paper.

Angelique cocked her head ever so slightly and twitched her index finger slightly in his direction letting him know that she was attentive and ready to receive his signals when he was ready.

While she wouldn't actually have called it a smile, the corners of his mouth turned slightly upward and he reached out his hand to cover hers.

"There's no need for that with Yo-Hyun." he said confirming her earlier suspicions. "He'll be your temporary bodyguard until I can hire a team."

"Sir …" Yo-Hyun interjected and was quickly cut off.

"No, it can not be a permanent assignment though I deeply appreciate your willingness to do so. I have no idea how reckless The Chairman will be and I will need you by my side."

Angelique's eyes grew wide and her lips formed an 'o'. She held her breath so that she didn't let out any audible sound. That brief exchange spoke volumes.

For starters, Yo-Hyun no longer referred to Seung-Hwa as 'Young Master'. That was a very clear indication that he no longer considered himself to be in her father's service but in her brother's. While she had always felt that to be true, there was no longer any pretense. The second was that her brother had referred to their father as 'The Chairman' rather than by filial terms.

Not that long ago she had wondered if he had been put in the middle between the two of them whether she could consider him an ally and take her side. She knew now without a doubt that she could count on him. She had to secretly admit to herself that it was a relief not to worry about protecting him as she had done during her most recent visit and confrontation with their father. It made her feel more confident and relaxed.

"Where are we heading?" she asked when she dared to breathe again.

"To look at apartments." He handed her several listings which he had printed out.

She scanned them briefly. She was once again reminded of their lifestyle differences as she did the quick 'drop three zeroes' conversion shortcut and noted that the cheapest apartment was $15,000 US dollars per month. None had fewer than seven bedrooms.

"Gangnam? Really? While I admit that it's fairly centrally located and has easy access to the subway line, it's not exactly something that I can afford on the salary that the network is paying me. All I need is a studio in any other district but Gangnam."

Seung-Hwa noticeably flinched at her mention of public transportation. He positively glared at her at the mention of a studio.

"In addition to being upscale rentals with all the amenities, these buildings have CCTV and on-staff security. You are far safer in one of them than anywhere else that you could stay. They are also within walking distance to my main office, which will allow me to check on you. Moreover, Yo-Hyun will be driving you to and from the network studio and site locations."

His posture and tone left no doubt that this was non-negotiable. She might have some small input about one of the half dozen that he had pre-selected but that would be the extent of it.

Angelique pouted. "I know. I am a Min and should conduct myself accordingly," she recited verbatim the litany that he had spent weeks trying to drill into her head.

Seung-Hwa twisted in his seat so that he faced her and took her hands in his. He knew that in her own way she was trying not to be an inconvenience and be independent. He appreciated her self-reliance but not at the risk of her safety.

His tone softened and when he spoke it was barely above a whisper. "Yeodongsaeng, despite what you might think, this is not about living as befits your station. Though I fully believe that you should. I have only had a brief time to get to know you, but you mean more to me than you will ever know or than I could ever express. In that short time, I have almost lost you twice. I simply am not willing to tempt the fates a third time."

Angelique reached out her hand, touched his cheek, and sighed in acquiescence. How could she possibly refute such a heart-felt argument like the one he had given when he was usually so guarded with his emotions?

Angelique's body language told Seung-Hwa that he had won the battle. However, while he was indeed used to getting his own way, 'winning' against his sister was no victory. He offered an olive branch.

"What if I take the apartment in my name as a convenience to be closer to the office? I will even stay there to keep up appearances. Since everyone believes you to be a distant cousin, it would not be improper for you to stay with me. But if it makes you feel more self-sufficient, you can pay me for the room at a rent equal to a place that you would have chosen for yourself."

"Can I bring Yoon-Suk? There would be more than enough room." she asked hopefully.

Seung-Hwa met Yo-Hyun's eyes in the rear-view mirror. His secretary subtly shook his head. He turned back to face her. "I don't think that's a good idea. I know that you like and trust her, but I can't be sure of her loyalties. She and her family are The Chairman's servants."

Angelique sighed once more in resignation and nodded her agreement.

EPISODE 6 – BAPTISM BY FIRE

Angelique stifled a yawn behind the back of her hand. Despite having been previously warned of the long hours involved in the production of a KDrama, she was not used to the daily marathon of meetings, interviews, cattle calls, and callbacks. The mountain of bios that had to be read, sorted, and scheduled never seemed to get any smaller. She yawned a second time. She decided that she needed yet another cup of coffee. It would be her fifth one so far today. She required its assistance to build up her stamina and endurance. 6 am was just too damn early to be expected to accomplish anything productive without it.

She had never really considered the tremendous amount of background work that went on behind the scenes of one of her beloved KDramas. The endless hours of meetings needed to work out schedules, not just of cast and crew but also dividing the workload of arrangements necessary for location shoots – securing the site, transportation of equipment, and lodging for everyone involved. Reviewing set designs and prop lists and their associated schedules, as well as the building and securing of same. All of this had to be done within a very limited budget.

She didn't even want to think about the amount of work that would still need to be done once production actually began – the blocking and marking, readings, and rehearsals before filming finally occurred. Post-production on earlier episodes would be done simultaneously as subsequent ones are being shot and the first ones being aired. If she thought that the pace was arduous now, she wondered how she would manage once they hit that point. She was coming to a completely new understanding of why burnout was so high in the Korean entertainment industry.

They were coming to the end of their second month of PREP (pre-production) and she could count on one hand the number of times that she had seen her brother. Though she would never tell him so, she was secretly grateful that he had insisted that Yo-Hyun drive her to and from work. She often fell asleep in the car during the ride back to the apartment and either he or Seung-Hwa had carried her to her room on more than one occasion. She didn't dare think about how a long subway commute both ways would have impacted her beauty sleep.

She wrapped both hands around her coffee mug and felt its warmth spread through her as she raised it to her lips to sip while reading the acting CV in front of her. This one was to be for the actor who played Seung-Hwa. For obvious reasons, that was not her brother's name in the book but it was how she kept personalities and looks in mind while conducting interviews. They had filled most of the cast, but choices for this one were proving difficult, especially because of the height requirement.

Like so many of the other applicants, there was no actual work experience in the field outside of school productions. This one was a business major at Seoul National University who was also pursing a minor in theater. His transcript showed that he probably would have enough credits to change that to a double major before graduation.

Park Ji-Tae. That name sounded so familiar, but she couldn't place it. She was sure that she had heard it before but it wasn't registering in her sleep deprived brain. She searched for his headshot that should have been attached but didn't find it. She lifted various papers on her table – you couldn't actually call it a desk - thinking that it had somehow gotten buried under something that she had moved. It probably had, but she wasn't able to find it. She asked the gofer to show him in.

She was still shuffling things around when he entered and greeted her. When she glanced up, she did a quick appraisal. Tall, dark brown wavy hair, dark brown eyes, unreadable expression. It bode well. She set her elbows on the table and laced her fingers, setting her chin on top of them as she scrutinized him further.

A hurt expression crossed his face. Mockingly he held his hand to his heart as if wounded, "You don't remember me? After everything that we meant to each other? I'm crushed." As she took a longer and closer look, her memory slammed her head against the brick wall that she had built there.

His hair color had been allowed to grow out or dyed back to its' natural color. He also had done his homework and gotten a perm for the part. He looked very different from when she had first met him and his friend in her brother's man cave. This was none other than the spiked bleached blonde who had been dressed edgy in black leather and looked like a KPop idol. The one that she had nicknamed 'bad boy.' The one that her father had chosen for her AMMA (arranged marriage of merger and acquisition) as a carrot to lure her away from Hyung-Joo in exchange for legally claiming her as his daughter and putting her on the family registry. Thankfully, he had never known that fact. Her father had never actually gotten into negotiations with Chairman Park.

"Aish…" She swore under her breath as she fumbled awkwardly to rise and bow, knowing that he was Chaebol. While she was technically his social superior and didn't need to do so, he only knew her to be a distant cousin and she needed to maintain that illusion.

Before she could fully stand, he closed the distance between them and took a seat in the chair next to hers, removing the paper stack which was piled there and carefully placing it neatly to the side. "No need for formalities with me. I am not as much a stickler for them as your cousin. Unless I don't like you." he winked at her.

Angelique was flustered. She had never expected to see this man again. He was the one who was supposed to be nervous since he was the one that wanted the part and she was the one who stood between him and a callback. But it was the exact opposite. How had the tables been turned? And how was it that the underlying personality trait of every Chaebol that she had ever met was cockiness?

Angelique found her voice, "Why?"

"Why, what? Do you mean why do I want the part when I don't really need it?"

"Exactly. Plus, we both know that this isn't a career path that Chairman Park is likely to allow you to pursue full time. So, why?"

Ji-Tae leaned back in his chair and rocked it onto its back two legs while swinging his feet up onto the table. Angelique wondered if he would have been so brazen if his interviewer had been anyone else besides herself.

"Bored, I suppose." he said inspecting his nails and flicking his thumbnail underneath another to clean some speck of imaginary dirt since they were impeccably manicured. "I mean, you're right, this isn't something that I have to do in order to put bread on the table but it is something that I enjoy and that I'm quite good at as you know from the letters of recommendation from my professors."

Angelique didn't know because she hadn't read them. Nor did she intend to let him know as much. She simply nodded assent. "Go on," she encouraged him to continue.

"Not much else to tell. You're also right that I will end up running the company eventually but I figured that I should have a little fun between now and then. Besides, I couldn't resist when I saw the headlines and knew whose drama it was." he winked at her for the second time in their brief time together. "How about putting in a good word for me? Besides, you owe me at least that much for forgetting me."

"I'll buy you an apple." Angelique promised earnestly using the Korean apology custom that developed because the two words – apple and apology – were homonyms in that language.

He laughed so heartily that he almost fell backwards in the chair. He swung his feet off the table and put all four of the chair legs on the ground. He leaned forward into her personal space. "Let me buy you lunch instead," he countered charmingly.

Angelique didn't understand why her heart had started to pound or why her face felt warm or why she was gripping the sides of her seat for dear life. She had to admit that he had the attitude of the character down pat. Whether or not that was an intentional performance, an inborn trait, one developed by environment, or any combination of the three, she neither knew nor cared.

She scooted her chair back and away from him and stood looking down at him. "I have a meeting." she said with as much composure as she could muster. She gathered the few things that she needed and started to walk away. She stopped when she was about twenty feet away and spoke over her shoulder, "I'll put your name on the callback list. Whether or not you get the part will depend on your reading with the director."

Ji-Tae watched her back as she headed for the door chuckling to himself. His interview with her was because he wanted the excuse to meet her again and had nothing whatsoever to do with the part. He would get the part because he wanted it and, because of who he was, it was guaranteed that he would get it.

"Raincheck?" he called after her hopefully.

Angelique hugged her notebook to her chest, doubled her pace, and pretended not to hear.

EPISODE 7 – FRIENDLY FIRE

Ji-Tae had indeed gotten the role for which he auditioned. Watching the tape of his reading, Angelique couldn't agree more that he was a good addition to the cast. She hadn't wished him ill, but she also had hoped that he wouldn't have been the best one for the part. It meant that she would be thrown together with him more than she would like. And he seemed to relish her discomfort when that happened. For example, he insisted on attending the English classes even though he had scored a 900 out of 990 in the Test of English for International Communication. He probably could have taught the subject. There was no reason for him to be there other than to have an excuse to be close to her. When confronted, he argued that it was in everyone else's schedule and he didn't want to create friction between the cast and crew who might get the impression that he thought that he was better than everyone else if he failed to attend. She disliked that it was such a plausible defense.

Even those unpleasant thoughts couldn't dampen her mood today. She pushed those replayed memories out of her mind and reviewed the schedule for the day. After almost three months of

PREP, they were going to start table reads. It would be the first time
that all the actors would be together, reading the script aloud, and
jotting down notes that the directors gave to them into their copies.
As if that wasn't enough reason to be happy, spring was in the air
and the cherry blossoms were budding and would soon come out.
However, the spring in her step wasn't just weather related. It was
mostly due to the text message that she had received at some point
while she was sleeping and had seen upon waking. Spring Break was
coming up and Hyung-Joo was going to be coming out to see her.

She was so busy daydreaming that she hadn't noticed that Ji-
Tae had fallen in step beside her.

"You have friends in some high places," he said passing her a
cup of coffee and hotteok having noticed that was her typical choice
each morning.

He was referring to the continuous 'can you top this' food
truck feud between Hyung-Joo and Seung-Hwa. It had begun with a
simple coffee service being delivered in her name by Hyung-Joo on
her first day of work. It was customary during KDrama filming that
friends (or even fans) express their support for each other
through sending a coffee or food truck to the set. It's a way of saying
they wish the drama success and smooth filming. She had thought it
a sweet gesture and it had warmed her heart that, while they were
physically distant, she was still very much in his heart. Not to be
outdone, her brother had ordered a lunch truck the following day.
The two had gotten carried away trying to outdo each other in both
quality and quantity. At least the staff was eating well.

"My understanding is that it has something to do with a
childhood rivalry." Angelique just shook her head at the childishness
of it. "Komowo," she called back holding the pastry up over her
head and waving it in her right hand as she kept walking toward her
destination.

Ji-Tae thought that it had to be something a bit more than that
but held his tongue. Seung-Hwa he could understand since
Angelique was a relative even if a distant one. Lee Hyung-Joo on the
other hand was a different story altogether. He had been the one to

start the cascade of events. How did he fit into the picture? No, he smelled something a bit fishy. He had an inkling and he intended to find out if it was true.

***

Because of work, Angelique had no more time to spend with Hyung-Joo than she had with Seung-Hwa. The only reason that she had gotten to be with him at all is that he had temporarily taken over Yo-Hyun's duties of being her chauffer and bodyguard. They took as much advantage of it as possible.

One evening on the way home, he pulled over and parked along the waterfront. Hundreds of cherry trees lined the sidewalk on either side creating a canopy of fluffy, pink clouds. They walked hand in hand down the paved path. A light breeze blew in off the water creating a flurry of pink snow.

Angelique stopped dead in her tracks. Looking at her, Hyung-Joo saw a mixture of fear and dread that he hadn't seen in her since her confrontation with her father.

"What's wrong?" he asked concerned.

"Isn't there a myth that couples caught in falling cherry blossoms have reached the end of their relationship like the trees have reached the end of their flowering season?"

Hyung-Joo noted that she was almost panicked by the thought and smiled warmly at her. He unlaced his fingers from hers and put both hands on her shoulders. He looked deeply into her eyes and lowered his lips to hers in a brief, soft kiss.

"Did that seem like a goodbye kiss to you?"

"Nope!" she squealed as she planted another quick kiss on his lips before spinning out of his hold and twirling, arms outstretched, amidst the supple, velvety, pale pastel pink petals.

Hyung-Joo smiled broadly, bringing out his dimples, as he watched her spin like a ballerina in the swirling mass of flowers and his heart melted. He marveled at how she found such immense joy in the simplest of things. He had learned so much from her of what was truly significant in life and the importance of capturing the moment. He too spread his arms wide and felt the blossoms wash over him.

***

Ji-Tae watched the scene unfold from his car parked across the street. While he couldn't hear any dialogue, none was needed to confirm his suspicions. "So that's how it is?" he said aloud to himself. "We'll just see how long that lasts." he smirked as he pulled the vehicle back out into traffic.

***

Ji-Tae entered the writer's room where a meeting was taking place. They were re-working some scenes to take advantage of the dazzling display of nature that was Cherry Blossom Festival. This meant that timelines within the story needed to be changed.

He held up two cardboard carry boxes – one with coffee and condiments; the other with sweet breads. "I figured that you would be too busy to eat, so I brought breakfast to you."

He began to dole them out around the table. He humbly accepted the thanks of each recipient in turn. In reality, he had used it as an excuse to glance at the script changes.

"Ahh, Cherry Blossom Festival. Mother Nature's signal of the end of one season and the beginning of another."

When he set Angelique's food and drink down in front of her, he leaned in closer than he needed to in order to whisper in her ear. Angelique felt his soft, warm breath as he confided, "The same can be true of relationships don't you think? Foreshadowing much?"

Angelique watched him go and realized that he had once again managed to unnerve her to the core. She became aware that she had broken out in goosebumps. She didn't know if they were from fear or excitement. She dreaded what the first might indicate for her and Hyung-Joo; she was equally as terrified of what the second might portend. She rubbed her arms to get rid of them. How is it that he managed to get under her skin almost every time they met?

EPISODE 8 – IN THE LINE OF FIRE

Ji-Tae noticed Angelique heading down the corridor that led to the sound studio. He supposed that she had been sent to check on how the soundtrack was coming. They were getting close to actual filming and the music would need to be ready when the first set of scenes went to editing and post-production. He checked his watch. He didn't have a ton of time before he needed to be in makeup and wardrobe, but he calculated that he could make it back by the skin of his teeth. He waited behind the door, listening carefully, and timed his exit from the bathroom so that he 'accidentally' collided with her in the small hallway.

Angelique was startled by his sudden appearance and screamed. "Oh my stars, you scared me half to death!" she exclaimed, breathing heavily and holding her hand to her heart. Her knees started to buckle and she leaned back against the wall for support lest her legs give out on her.

Ji-Tae seized the opportunity to close the distance between them. He leaned into her personal space and placed his two hands on the wall on either side of her head. His face was mere inches from hers.

Angelique's heart raced and she felt the blush creep into her cheeks. They locked eyes and even though everything in her being was screaming to look away she found that she couldn't. Her voice was hoarse and barely audible, "Are you going to kiss me?"

Ji-Tae winked at her and smiled. "Why? Do you want me to?"

"No!" she eeked.

"Then why ask?" he demanded with a smirk, continuing to hold her gaze and not blinking.

Angelique tried to bring herself up to her full stature but found that she was unable to do so with the way that Ji-Tae had his hands placed. She brought her ring up to her face, blocking his lips from hers, "I'm engaged!" she declared as she swallowed hard.

Ji-Tae had already noticed the ring months before. The heart shaped stone was a deep green. Most people would think that it was an emerald from its intense dark color, but Ji-Tae knew it to be a very rare and supremely high quality green diamond. He estimated it to be somewhere around three carats. He wondered whether or not she realized that the piece of jewelry that she wore so carelessly was worth upwards of a half billion won.

"He's my soul mate!" Angelique's voice was a little stronger than before but still not quite normal.

"You don't seem to know much about our culture. We believe that people have different soul mates at different times of their lives."

He watched Angelique struggle to digest that piece of information and pressed his advantage, "Shall we check and see if we are soul mates?" He moved his hand to place it over her heart as she had described in her book. That, in turn, had been taken from a classic K-Drama. In *Doctor Stranger*, Park Hoon had held his hand over Song Jae-hee's heart and told her that no two hearts beat the same except for those of soul mates. He then took hers and placed it over his.

Upon hearing this, Angelique finally found her resolve. "And you, dear boy, don't seem to know much about the genre in which you are acting. Rule #1 of the Laws of the KDrama Universe: The second male lead *never* gets the girl! " She ducked under his arm and beat a hasty retreat.

Ji-Tae leaned back against the same wall that Angelique had been propped up against and stared after her with an amused expression on his face, wondering, not for the first time, "Exactly who the hell are you Angelique Randolph?"

He caught motion out of his peripheral vision and turned his head in time to see Hyung-Joo storm off down a side corridor, his hands balled into fists.

Ji-Tae pursed his lips and stuck his tongue in his cheek. "So he caught at least part of our little tryst, did he? This is about to get r-e-a-l interesting!" He cackled to himself as he stuck both hands in his pockets and sauntered off to his dressing room.

EPISODE 9 – CAUGHT IN THE CROSS FIRE

Filming had begun and, though Angelique hadn't thought it possible, things were even busier and more hectic than before. She was racing across the lot to get the latest script changes to the filming studio when she saw Ji-Tae standing nearby the latest and most elaborate edition of food truck central. She called it 'central' because there were now so many being delivered that they were assigned equidistant locations so that you were never far from a fueling station. She had been avoiding him like the plague since their encounter in the hallway but there was something about his demeanor that was 'off' and made her hesitate.

She couldn't quite place her finger on it. She had been in a hurry so she had to take a moment to calm herself. She was an excellent people watcher. She had honed the skill through high school to the present as she trained to be an investigative reporter. His face and eyes were blank. He was hyper-focused on whatever it was that he held in his hands. He wasn't exactly staring at it; he was staring beyond it. It was as if various possible scenarios were being broadcast in his head. He didn't exude his usual haughty aura. His shoulders were slightly slumped indicating what? Defeat? Sadness? What?

Her curiosity got the best of her. While she didn't like that he seemed to take great delight in making her feel uncomfortable whenever they were together, she didn't think that would be a problem today. He really looked like he needed a friend. She was reminded of the stark similarity between him and her brother in that respect. Chaebol had no true friends – only business acquaintances. Angelique's heart softened a great deal towards the man for whom she had, until now, felt a great deal of animosity. She thought that maybe if she extended the first offer of a truce that they could get back onto some type of equal footing.

Whatever was bothering him had him almost in a trance. He didn't even realize that she was standing right in front of him. She couldn't miss what he was holding. She spoke to him quietly and calmly as she would to an injured animal to let him know that she was there. She laid a reassuring hand on his until he relinquished his death grip on the lurid, incriminating photos of him and his lover. Angelique replaced them in the envelope in which they had been delivered and placed them in the pocket on the inside of his jacket. She patted it to let him know that both the evidence and he were now protected. "Your secret is safe with me. I promise." she whispered softly.

Ji-Tae placed his hand over hers on his chest. He clenched her small hand as desperately as he had held the pictures. His eyes sought hers forlornly. "Nugu?"

It was a barely audible, deeply guttural cry for help. If she hadn't been so near she would not have heard him ask "Who?" Angelique feared that she knew the answer to that one. It had not been so long ago that both she and her brother had been in his shoes. She wasn't sure which Chairman was responsible, but either way this was her fault. They were going to take down the drama and everyone involved in it to get to her. No entertainment undertaking wants the publicity of a negative scandal such as this one.

"I don't know for sure, but I can guess. Jwesong hamnida. People with friends in high places usually have enemies there as well. You're getting caught in the cross fire. Jwesong hamnida." she apologized again.

Ji-Tae read the sincerity in her eyes and knew that they had bonded in a way that he had never intended but was grateful for nonetheless. Angelique felt it also. They had found their armistice.

They were still sharing that moment when the reporters pushed her to the side and started shoving mics into Ji-Tae's face. "Is it true that you're having an illicit affair with one of your co-stars?"

Angelique briefly wondered which one of the security guards had been bribed to allow them on the set. The thought didn't last long as she caught Ji-Tae's eyes desperately pleading for help. Angelique once again felt the deep burden of responsibility for his predicament. She had made the promise to keep him safe and protect his secret but she was at a complete and utter loss as to how to do it.

"Aish …" she closed her eyes tightly, shook her head, stomped her feet.

She didn't stop to think about her actions. If she had, she wondered whether she would have done the same thing. She elbowed her way back into the position that she had been in when she had been so rudely thrust aside. She grabbed Ji-Tae's necktie, pulled his face down to hers, and planted a passionate kiss on his lips.

Ji-Tae was shocked, eyes wide. It only lasted a moment. He raised his suit jacket to cover their faces and block the flashes that were incessantly popping. He scooped her up into his arms and, shielding her as best he could, ran into the nearest building.

***

Hyung-Joo had watched nearby as the scene unfolded. He clenched and unclenched his fists in ire. Then he went to find a back way into the building since the front was layers deep in reporters. He wanted answers.

***

When Hyung-Joo found them, they were in the cubicle that served as Angelique's office, such as it was. She was in Ji-Tae's lap sobbing into his chest. He had his arms around her, consoling her.

Hyung-Joo cleared his throat. His stance was cold and distant. His jaw set and firm. The veins in his neck and temples were throbbing. "Explain yourself!" he demanded.

Angelique suddenly realized the compromising position that she was in and jumped to her feet, wiping away her tears as she did so.

"It's not what it looks like," Ji-Tae started.

"I don't want to hear anything from you." he spat, glancing momentarily at Ji-Tae, then he stared long and hard at Angelique.

She ran toward him to throw her arms around him but he stepped back and away from her. She was dumfounded and stopped dead in her tracks. He had never refused her affections.

"It's not what you think." she reiterated.

"Then exactly what is it? I'm waiting." he responded brusquely, his body rigid.

"I …." she faltered and looked back at Ji-Tae who was slumped over with his head in his hands, his palms pressed hard against his eyes. It was the same thing that she used to do to stop herself from crying when she was a kid. She turned back to Hyung-Joo with imploring eyes. "I can't tell you. I made a promise."

Hyung-Joo didn't waver in his stance or in his tone, "You made one to me as well. Or have you forgotten?" His eyes moved to her engagement ring and he nailed home his point, "Just who do you think those reporters are going to believe put that little bauble on your finger? Any contact between the two of us now would be considered highly improper. One scandal is enough for any drama."

Angelique bit her lip. Her heart ached at the pain that she saw etched on his face. Pain that she had inflicted. Tears welled in her eyes and fell silently down her cheeks. She wondered how she was going to write her way out of this one. "I'm so sorry Oppa. Truly I am. I didn't think." She once more advanced toward him and he once more retreated.

"You never do." he replied softly and sadly. "I'll inform Yo-Hyun that he will need to pick you up." Hyung-Joo turned sharply on his heels and departed.

Ji-Tae opened his arms to welcome her and she curled up into a ball in his lap. Angelique knew without him saying it that he was thankful that she kept her promise and protected him. He knew without her saying it that she knew that his silence wasn't driven by self-preservation. He too was protecting someone. All that was in his power was to hold her protectively until she had cried herself to sleep.

***

The sasaeng and netizens made sure that the videos and photos kept the top ten search spots on the internet occupied by *Off Seoul Searching* for weeks afterwards. Moreover, everyone eagerly awaited the airing of the first episode of the drama, speculating on whether or not it would be as good as the gossip that accompanied it.

***

Half a world away, Danielle Randolph read the tabloids and wondered what on earth had happened that made her daughter deviate from the path that she had faithfully followed until now. She slammed the lid of her laptop closed in exasperation. "Child, make up your damn mind!" She picked up her phone and started placing calls to find out the backstory.

EPISODE 10 – OPEN FIRE

Seung-Hwa approached his father's ornately carved antique desk. The wood gave off a warm glow from both its highly polished sheen and the reflection of the fire from the hearth. The scene was postcard worthy. However, a bitter chill hung in the air that had nothing to do with the thermometer reading of the room.

He had respected and admired his father for most of his life. He had firmly stood up for him and by him through everything. He had pushed everyone and everything out of his life in order to make his father proud and prove himself a worthy heir. He had done it willingly and without remorse. Until now.

Once he had rescued Angelique, their relationship had become strained at best. Seung-Hwa wasn't sorry if that was the price that had to be paid for a relationship with his sister. He would not be the first or only Chaebol offspring to be estranged from their parents.

They had managed to continue to conduct business with no difficulty but they carefully maneuvered around the taboo subject of his sister. Neither of them had spoken of the incident at the airport nor were they ever likely to do so. They had drawn their boundaries and neither crossed into the other's territory.

Before he had moved out, Seung-Hwa and his father had shared breakfast every morning and dinner each evening. It was during that time that they kept up to date on each other's lives. In retrospect, Seung-Hwa realized that they had never really discussed anything of any real consequence.

He did away with any unnecessary pleasantries and got right to the point, "Why did you rescind my approval for the filming at our hotel on Jeju-do?"

Chairman Min was a heavy-set, middle-aged man with deep creases around his eyes and jowls. Despite his age, he still had the same dark wavy hair that he had in his youth unaltered by salon products. He leaned back in his chair and folded his hands above his portly belly. His upper lip curled with disdain.

"I didn't realize that I needed your permission to conduct the business of my establishments." he cocked his eyebrow.

"You don't. I have never questioned any of your business decisions. But this one is not sound practice. They are paying standard group rates for the rooms that they booked and top dollar for the event facilities and grounds. We aren't being asked for sponsorship, so it isn't costing the company a dime. If anything, it is free advertising."

Seung-Hwa wanted to add that he was being petty and vindictive but that wouldn't have been at all productive if he wanted to sway his father's opinion on the matter. He knew that he had to keep to the facts if he were to get anywhere with him on this subject.

He knew that many corporate executives abused their wealth and power and knew that his father was as manipulative as the next in that respect but he had never known his father to ignore a good business opportunity for the sake of revenge.

"I don't have to explain my reasoning for those decisions either." The Chairman replied matter-of-factly.

"You would rather that the product placement and business go to LH Group?" he tried to gain leverage by appealing to his father's competitive side and long standing rivalry with Chairman Lee.

"You think that Chairman Lee wants his conglomerate associated with this drama anymore than I do? I doubt that they will find any accommodations whatsoever on the island."

Seung-Hwa was at a loss. His father had not risen to take the bait of either of his appeals - financial gain or competition. He was being completely ruthless in his personal vendetta against his sister. His comment left little doubt that he intended for the drama to be blacklisted.

He wished that he had more intel regarding the recent scandal incident. He had no doubt at this juncture that his father was behind it somehow since he had exhausted all other avenues.

He had asked Angelique directly and she had told him that she couldn't explain because she had made a promise to Ji-Tae. She said that she had made a rash decision that seemed logical at the time. She admitted that she hadn't thought about the ramifications of her actions. She had cried profusely and it broke his heart to see her so unhappy. She hadn't taken her ring off so he knew that her heart had not changed. He also knew this to be true because he listened to her cry herself to sleep every night.

Then he had thought that perhaps Ji-Tae had some hold over her. Ji-Tae denied the allegation but Seung-Hwa wouldn't have expected him to admit it. They had even gotten into a physical altercation over the matter. In the end, Seung-Hwa ended up believing him that he wasn't blackmailing Angelique but he also felt that Ji-Tae definitely knew a lot more than he was telling. The cryptic comment of 'just the opposite' was his only clue.

Hyung-Joo and Jessica knew less than he did. He added what little more he had garnered to their database. Collectively they concluded that for reasons known only to her, Angelique was protecting Ji-Tae and probably the drama as well.

Seung-Hwa looked at his father and wondered what hold he had over Chairman Park's son. But, staring into those cold, calculating eyes, he finally realized just how right Angelique had been about him.

This was never going to end. His father was going to continue to make her life miserable along with those around her until she had felt the full measure of his wrath and he had exacted every ounce of pleasure that he could from the experience. Simply because she existed which had never been in his plans. Because he was spiteful and malicious.

Seung-Hwa thought about his sister's fortitude in her recent confrontation with him. He knew, in this moment, that although she had won that battle, she would never truly win the war. It had only been the fact that Angelique approached life from an extremely chaotic core belief system that she had managed to best him last time. It would only be a matter of time before he found some way to crush her completely. He could not bear the thought of the emotional struggles and damage to her spirit that his sister would have to endure before that happened.

He fleetingly toyed with the idea of dropping to his knees and begging him to leave her alone. If for no other reason than for his sake. But he knew with certainty that would be seen as a sign of weakness and met with contempt. It was a rude awakening for him to realize that his sister meant absolutely nothing to him even though she was his own flesh and blood. He had to wonder what role he truly played in his father's life and affections other than being a carefully crafted heir.

He opted for a direct approach. "Exactly what will it take to get you to back off and leave her alone? Name your price."

Chairman Min had watched his son's face carefully. While his son was quite adept at keeping a passive expression, Angelique had turned out to be his Achilles Heel. She had made him soft. Though his son was calm and collected in his demeanor, he could tell that a torrent of emotions raged within him. He could see the wheels turning as his son formulated, calculated, and discarded various solutions to the problem at hand. He was glad to see that he was intelligent enough to know that all scenarios eventually spelled disaster for all parties concerned.

He knew that his son was never going to let the matter rest. Short of his son's or Angelique's demise, this was going to continue to be a wedge that would only be driven deeper, dividing them and creating more distance between them.

Angelique's response to what should have been a major exposé had been totally unforeseen. Despite that, she had unwittingly played into the hand that he had previously dealt to her and to which she had folded.

"I've already answered that question once. However, since you seem to have forgotten, I will remind you. Agree to let me approach Chairman Park to offer a double AMMA between you and Park Eun-Chae and between Park Ji-Tae and that bastard child that you insist on calling your sister. She seems to have made her decision, what is yours?"

Seung-Hwa had known that the price would not be monetary. Nevertheless, it was a heavy wager. He had to choose between his sister and the woman he loved. Before he had confessed to Jessica, he had known and accepted that an arranged marriage of merger and acquisition was in his future. He had allowed himself to believe that he could change his destiny. Angelique had given him that hope. However, his sister's world was not the one that he lived in. It was not reality.

He looked once more into his father's devious and conniving eyes. He understood now that Hyung-Joo was not going to be able to protect her from this man despite his willingness to do so regardless of the wealth and power his family possessed. The only one with the ability to do that was he. He prayed to the ancestors that both of the women in his life would forgive him.

Seung-Hwa had to swallow the lump in his throat and hardened his heart so that his voice was steady and firm. His eyes never wavered from his fathers. "Call."

EPISODE 11 – BREATHING FIRE

Angelique returned to the apartment late into the evening as was typical these days. Filming was well underway with the first episode set to air in a couple weeks. They would be leaving for Jeju-do in the morning. Late as it was, she still had to pack for the trip.

There had been a period of several days where it looked as if they wouldn't be able to film on location. When she told her brother about the studio's difficulties in securing a site, he had said that he would take care of it. Obviously, he had.

She slipped her shoes off inside the door, as was the normal Korean custom. Her brother insisted that it wasn't necessary at their caste level since the staff would take care of cleaning up any mess that would be made. Her brother had been raised that way; she had not. Moreover, she never wanted to get into the habit of treating people as inferiors.

She went down the short hallway that was set with alcoves displaying numerous sculptures from artisans both living and dead. It opened up to an expansive open floor plan containing the living room, dining area, and kitchen.

She stopped short when she saw a strange woman sitting on the sofa. She was reading a magazine and making notes in a leather planner. Angelique noted that she was petite and drop-dead gorgeous. Her skin was flawless; her hair, long and luxurious. The woman slightly turned her head in her direction. Long thick lashes framed her double lidded, almond shaped eyes.

Angelique wondered if she was interested in acting. She so had the look of a female lead. She came a little further into the room, bowed a full 90 degrees, and formally introduced herself in Korean.

The woman didn't rise. Though her face never registered anything, her eyes shot daggers in Angelique's direction. Her voice, when she spoke, was viperous. "I know well who you are."

Angelique wondered what the hell she had done to offend this total stranger. Her brother made sure that security was tight around their inner sanctum. Whoever this was, she was a significant person to her brother. She began to apologize for any unintentional slight.

"You have no idea who I am, do you?" The tone didn't change and she punctuated it with a 'pfft'.

Angelique wracked her brain but, try as she might, she couldn't recall ever seeing this woman before in her life.

"The name is Park Eun-Chae," she prompted.

Recollection dawned on Angelique's face. "Oh! You're Ji-Tae's sister! Hi!" she said with a wide, beaming smile as she started across the floor towards her and continued, "Your brother's very talented. We got off on the wrong foot at first, but he's pretty okay. I hope we can be friends." Angelique extended her hand.

The woman stood for the first time and slapped her hand away. She sneered at Angelique. "Be glad that wasn't your face." she spat.

Angelique was flabbergasted. The astonishment on her face must have been apparent because the woman quickly followed it up with, "You really don't remember, do you?"

Angelique thought that she seemed to have a habit of forgetting the members of that family. She wondered if it were Freudian. Though she had quickly recognized Ji-Tae, she truly had no memory of the woman in front of her. She shook her head, 'no'.

Eun-Chae scoffed at her, "I *was* – past tense - the fiancé of Lee Hyung-Joo that got jilted at her own engagement party while he went to rescue some damned fool Cinderella wannabe." She would have added the rest but Seung-Hwa had made it crystal clear that he was to be the one to break the news. She knew that she wasn't married yet and didn't dare cross him. Yet.

Angelique felt as if she had been punched in the gut. *That* was what her father had meant when he had said that she was getting the better end of the bargain when he had discussed the double

AMMA with her in private. He hadn't been trying to pit her against Seung-Hwa as she had supposed. Eun-Chae's reputation, and therefore desirability as a partner choice, had been sullied. In their world, she was 'used goods.'

Horror washed through her. She hoped against hope that this woman's presence in the house didn't portend what she was thinking. She turned tail and ran to find her brother.

Eun-Chae smiled a malevolent Cheshire Cat grin at Angelique's retreating figure.

***

"You did WHAT??!!?? WHY??!!?? W-T-F Oppa??!!??" had been Angelique's reaction when Seung-Hwa gave her the news. Jessica's response before disconnecting the video call had simply been "I understand." He had not given either one the full story. Seung-Hwa despised himself for the deep suffering that he was causing to both of them. Still, he didn't see any other possible recourse. Though they couldn't see it, this was best for both of them. He hung his head in his hands and cried silent, bitter tears.

EPISODE 12 – FIRE IN THE HOLE

Angelique was placing props on the set. One thing that she had learned very quickly in her experience thus far while working on this KDrama is that you wore many hats. They truly were team efforts. It didn't matter what your job title was or what your job description entailed. If there was a need somewhere and you were available, you rolled up your sleeves and pitched in.

She heard the sound of screeching metal just before she was forcefully shoved out of harms way. Either the truss hadn't been secured properly or wasn't sufficient to handle the weight it bore and had come crashing down to the floor from several stories above with several hundred pounds of audio visual and lighting equipment.

She picked herself up off the floor where she had landed with an unceremonious 'plop' and dusted herself off. The male crew members had gathered around the spot and were frantically working to remove debris. They had set up a type of bucket brigade to clear the area. Muscles strained to pass the heavy metal pieces. She heard one of them yell to dial 119. Someone had to be seriously injured if they were calling for an ambulance.

She ran forward to offer what help she could. Her mother was a nurse and had made sure that she was a certified first responder in the States. She normally reacted well in a medical crisis and only fell apart afterwards as she thought about all the things that could have gone wrong. However, today she found that she was physically paralyzed and numb from fear and couldn't move a muscle because her savior who was lying there bleeding and battered was Hyung-Joo.

"Ottoke?" was all she could manage to say.

***

Angelique and Seung-Hwa waited anxiously in the hospital VIP waiting room. She had called Jessica who was on her way via the company's private jet. This was probably the first and only time that she was thankful for the fact that her family had more money than sense.

Angelique was beside herself with worry. She kept twisting the ends of her hair so that her hands had something to do. She had thought that he had gone back to the US after he had left her and Ji-Tae. She took hope from the fact that he had stuck around to mean that they could work things out. She was grateful that he had saved her. However, she was once again reminded of how much those that she loved suffered because of her.

They were overjoyed when the doctor told them that he would be fine. He had severe deep bruising but the duplex ultrasonography had showed no signs of resulting blood clots. He had only a mild concussion. The doctor said that it was miraculous that was all the injuries that he had sustained. Angelique cried in relief.

They were told that they could go in to see him but only for a short time so that he didn't become overexerted.

***

Angelique's heart hurt deeply when she saw the bruises on his face. It hurt even more when he barked, "What the hell are you doing here?"

Angelique's knees buckled and Seung-Hwa instinctively threw his arm around her waist to keep her from collapsing. She wondered exactly what she expected considering the last exchange that they had.

Hyung-Joo noticed the heart-shaped green diamond on her finger. When he spoke, his voice was alien to Angelique's ears. "Come to gloat that your father allowed you to keep your plaything from Jeju-do after all? Congrats. Now get out."

That was when they realized that he had been talking to Seung-Hwa and not to Angelique. The two looked at each other in deep concern and buzzed for the doctor.

***

The diagnosis was dissociative amnesia. The doctors explained that it occurs when a person blocks out certain information, often associated with a stressful or traumatic event, leaving the person unable to remember important personal information. They said that it could last minutes or hours. They added that if it lasted longer than that it would most likely be months or years. There was also a possibility that it could be permanent.

Hyung-Joo seemed to remember Seung-Hwa but not that their relationship had changed. He remembered nothing about Angelique at all except that she had been Seung-Hwa's date during his 21st birthday celebration weekend. Jessica's name didn't strike any chord with him either.

Angelique leaned against her brother for support and buried her head in his chest. She wanted to cry but the tears wouldn't come. It was as if she had been emotionally anesthetized. She rued the day that she and Jessica had developed the Laws of the KDrama Universe because Hyung-Joo was currently experiencing Rule #22 - Every Chaebol will have amnesia at least once in their lifetime.

She frantically searched her memory banks for KDramas with that plot twist and ways that she could bring him back as he had done for her when she was in a coma. The few she tested in the room were ultimately met with 'get your bat shit crazy girlfriend out of here.' Every other possibility that she thought of was discarded as not applicable to this situation. She had nothing. She had never felt so helpless in her life.

    ***

Chairman Lee was berating the nurses for their refusal to allow him admittance to see his son while the doctors were assessing him.

As they passed him in the hallway and bowed a formal greeting, Angelique raised her head from where it rested on her brother's arm long enough to say, "Be patient. You'll be extremely happy with the results of their examination."

***

The stage manager declared it a freak accident. Angelique knew better. It was supposed to have been her. And she knew who was responsible.

***

Yo-Hyun was awoken from a beautiful dream in which he was bass fishing in Gosam Lake Reservoir by the incessant buzzing of the track phone. He bolted upright and checked the message – IMPLEMENT FINAL STAGE - and attachments.

EPISODE 13 – BURNING BRIDGES

Angelique was let into the manor house by Yoon-Suk. Her former personal maid seemed to have been elevated in station. The girl with whom she had bonded and shared many a pleasant time was now cold, distant, and proper. Her manner held no hint of their previous closeness or remorse at switching loyalties. Angelique knew that it was sheer self-preservation as Park Eun-Chae would soon be her new mistress. That didn't mean that it didn't sting.

Seung-hwa had temporarily returned to his old room so that Jessica would not feel uncomfortable by his presence. She had remained in Seoul to be with Angelique. She was finishing her semester remotely. Seung-Hwa knew that each was undergoing deep emotional suffering and was grateful that the two best friends had each other for support at this time.

Yo-Hyun remained with the girls at the apartment along with two additional bodyguards that her brother had hired. One for each of them. Angelique had asked Yo-Hyun to bring her by after work. He had wanted to come in with her but she said that she wanted to talk to her brother alone. He had nodded his understanding.

Eun-Chae had also moved into the main house to begin her bride training where she would learn her future husband's likes and dislikes so that she could better serve him after the nuptials. Angelique was glad that she saw no signs of her as she made her way to her brother's office.

She knocked tentatively but didn't wait for him to call for her to enter before opening the door and stepping inside. She made sure to close it fully so there would be no chance for anything they said to be overheard. She knew that the carved ebony double doors were very soundproof. She knew because she had on more than one occasion tried to eavesdrop through them.

Seung-hwa got up from his chair and moved from behind his desk to greet her. He hugged her closely and tightly. He was very worried about her. She was very pale and seemed to be losing weight. Some of that could be contributed to the number of hours that she worked but he knew that most of it was from her break-up with Hyung-Joo and his medical state.

He was scared for her. She looked worse than that dreadful night where she had slipped off the curb into oncoming traffic. At least that night her eyes had searched for him. There had still been emotion in them. Today her eyes were dull, with no spark of life within. They were bloodshot and puffy. He didn't know if that were from crying or stress or both. 'I'm just tired.' she had responded when he asked. He didn't know if that exhaustion was physical, mental, emotional, or a combination of the three. He led her to the sofa so they could sit. She looked as if she might collapse at any moment.

"I …" they both began at the same time.

"You first," he said.

"I want you to look me in the eye and tell me that you don't love Jessica."

"Did she send you?" Seung-Hwa wasn't sure why that was what he asked because he really wasn't sure that he wanted to know the answer to that. It was best if Jessica forgot all about him.

Angelique shook her head slightly to indicate 'no.'

"We both knew when we went into …"

"That's not what I asked and you know it." she cut him off knowing what the second half of the sentence was going to be before he even finished it. "Oppa, I don't have the energy to argue with you right now. Just answer my question. Jebal."

Seung-Hwa lowered his head and sighed, "I don't…"

She didn't allow him to continue. "Damn it! Don't look at the floor! I said look me in the eye and tell me!"

Seung-Hwa raised his eyes to meet hers. He opened his mouth but "I …" was all that came out. There was no sense in lying.

Though no one else could see past his stoic façade, his sister could read him like a book. He just stopped.

"That's what I thought. You did it for me, didn't you?"

Seung-Hwa didn't answer, but he didn't need to. She already knew. She knew her brother's heart. Therefore, she knew his AMMA was a deal that he had made in exchange for something that was important to him. The only thing in his life that might be more important to him than Jessica was she. It was highly suspicious to her that all of the location shoot problems mysteriously disappeared after he had told her that he would handle the matter.

She lowered her head and placed it in her hands, her palms pressing hard against her temples where they pounded with the perpetual headache that she seemed to have these days. Damn Korean men and their self-sacrificing, noble bullshit. She had to fix this. She rose to go.

"One more thing. I want Yoon-Suk gone." she told him flatly. She held her index finger up to his face, "And don't you dare tell me that you told me so."

Seung-Hwa nodded his assent. "I'll call her in and fire her immediately after you leave."

"That isn't what I said."

"Then … what?" a furrow appeared between his brows as he wondered what he had missed.

Angelique pushed the index finger that she had just waggled at him on the pressure point between his eyes. "Hajima. You'll get wrinkles on that handsome face of yours." She patted his cheek.

She met his gaze directly. "Both her parents have faithfully been in your employ for over a decade. There is no sense in having them lose face for the actions of their daughter. Reward the family for their service. Award her a scholarship and send her abroad to study. But I don't ever want to see her face again." She kissed his cheek and let herself out.

Seung-Hwa stared at the door long after she had closed it behind her. His sister was fiercely loyal to those that she took into her inner circle. She expected the same in return. He wondered why he worried about her. She had just now illustrated just how dangerous she could be if crossed.

***

"A word, if you please?" Angelique asked after bowing to her father and taking a seat across from his desk. Back when she was actually trying to please him, she had knelt in his presence. There didn't seem to be much sense in that at this point.

Chairman Min leaned back in his chair and crossed his arms and waited. Angelique knew that his stare was supposed to intimidate her. Once upon a time, it had. No longer.

"That was supposed to be me beneath that pile of rubble, wasn't it?" she asked without preliminary.

"Would you believe me if I said 'no'?" he answered her question with one of his own.

Angelique shook her head, "Absolutely not."

He wasn't surprised. He had already had this conversation with his son. He had managed to convince Seung-Hwa that he had no part in the accident that had occurred on the set. Fortunately, the wedge between them wasn't so wide as to allow him to think his father capable of murder.

Angelique was busy playing with the baby's breath in the arrangement on the end table next to her. It appeared to Chairman Min that she was far away and deep in thought so it surprised him when she spoke. She never took her eyes off the flowers and spoke with a dream like quality.

"Let my brother marry Jessica and I'll marry Ji-Tae."

He cackled to himself internally. This was just too perfect. The two of them trying to protect each other. How sweet. Except that neither of them was up to the task.

"Why should I do that?"

Angelique plucked the magnolia from its vase. She traced her finger along the petals feeling their softness as she drank in their strong fragrance. She realized that she was homesick. She loved what she was doing and she loved Seoul but a part of her would always miss the rural, deep South. Right now she longed for a sweet tea on the back porch swing with the song of the cicadas and the velvet black night filled with stars. She spoke from the same distant place.

"Because it's my life you want to ruin; not his."

"My son has always known that he was destined for an AMMA and has always accepted that fact. Whether you understand or accept our cultural traditions makes no difference. And, as I see it, I already have exactly what I offered you months ago so there is no reason for me to strike any type of deal with you."

Angelique broke off a piece of stem, fished a hairpin from her purse, and fixed the flower to the side of her head so that it covered her ear. She sat back and folded her arms across her chest.

She had read somewhere that mirroring an individual's actions increases rapport and liking from the other person. She no longer cared whether her father liked her or not but if it helped just a little to sway things in her direction then so much the better.

"Except that you don't. You will never have your double AMMA. I will never marry Ji-Tae unless my brother is allowed to marry the woman he loves. The gossip rags can speculate all they want. Talk doesn't make it happen. Only I can do that."

"Why would you do that?" he asked, genuinely curious.

"You wouldn't understand." Angelique sighed sadly.

"Try me."

"You are Seung-Hwa's father. While that might not mean anything more to you than an heir for your financial empire, it means a great deal more to him. He genuinely loves you. The only reason that he doesn't verbalize it is because he's convinced that you would think that any admission of affection would be a sign of weakness. And finally, though most importantly, I don't want to see my brother hurt. I don't want to see him miserable for the rest of his life because he was forced into a loveless marriage. Especially not because of me."

He decided to test her. "If you are finally ready to forsake Lee Hyung-Joo, give me the ring."

She twisted the ring in circles around her finger. She hadn't forsaken him. She still loved him deeply and wanted nothing more than to be with him. But the hours or days the doctors had spoken of had turned into months without change. Though she would never forget him, she had to accept that he had erased her from his life. She could be content without him and find solace in her writing, but she would never truly be happy. One of them deserved to marry for love. Let it be her brother. Not long ago she believed that both of them could be with the ones that they had chosen rather than ones that were chosen for them. But so much had happened between then and now.

Angelique slipped the ring off her finger and held it between her index finger and thumb. She had made a promise that she would never take it off again. Could she be held accountable for breaking a promise that her love didn't even remember asking her to make?

She held the ring in the space between them, "You can have it if you really want but how will I explain its' absence when all of Korea thinks that Ji-Tae is the one who put it there?" She stared him down the way that he had taught her.

In the end, Chairman Min allowed her to keep the ring. He also, for the first time, admitted that she was right. He didn't understand her reasons. There was no logic behind them at all. But he didn't need to understand them if they got him what he wanted. By allowing Seung-Hwa to marry that commoner, he would remain in high esteem in his sons' eyes. It would go up even more by putting that brat he called a sister on the family registry. Those two events would be scandalous for sure and temporarily affect stock market prices but the AMMA would securely move both families up the rungs of the social ladder. And, best of all, the fire had gone out of that bastard's eyes. That alone was worth making the trade.

They spent the next hour ironing out the timetable and details of how it would all happen to each other's satisfaction.

***

Angelique had Yo-Hyun drive her to Ji-Tae's apartment. Once there she told him her secret so that he understood why his was almost revealed. She also told him the deal that she had made with her father. He listened sympathetically, patting her hand as she talked.

He brushed back the wisps of hair that had fallen into her eyes. He lifted her chin so that she could meet his eyes. "Are you sure about this?"

Angelique nodded somberly.

Ji-Tae leaned in to kiss her and she pulled away. He laughed, "You really don't think things through before acting, do you?"

"Don't make fun of me." She stood to go.

He reached out and caught her wrist to stop her from leaving. He stood up beside her and looked deep into her eyes, "I wasn't making fun of you. Honest. It's just …." He stopped, unsure how to proceed.

"Just what?"

"We're going to be expected to produce an heir. That's going to be pretty tough if you won't even let me kiss you."

The look of horror that crossed her face as that realization struck home would have been comical if not for the circumstances. 'Way to give a guy a complex' he thought.

Angelique was puzzled. "But …"

He knew what she was going to say. "I know. We'll work it out somehow." he replied to her unanswered question as he pulled her close into a protective hug and kissed the top of her head.

Everything that Angelique had been holding in finally found its way to the surface. The dam broke and she trembled violently as deep sobs wracked her tiny frame. "Gwenchana," he cooed repeatedly until she was all cried out.

***

Angelique had a difficult time getting Jessica and Seung-Hwa to agree to be in the same room together. Both of them thought that it would only make matters worse. She knew that it wouldn't but she couldn't tell them that up front. It may have been easier to tell them separately but she didn't want to have to repeat everything twice and listen to the objections twice. The tension in the air was palpable.

It didn't get any better when she told them the arrangement she had made with her father. She sat quietly and let them get out everything they had to say out of their system before she told them her thought processes and gave them the same explanation that she had given her father. Another round of protests ensued about why she shouldn't go through with it.

The warmth in Angelique's heart spread to her face and she smiled for the first time in ages. It was a small one, but it was a real one nonetheless. Not the fake one that she plastered on at work so that no one would know that anything was wrong. They had teamed up together and ganged up on her. There was nothing like a common enemy to bring people together. She said as much.

She took advantage of their stunned silence to continue, "You do realize that we have sat here for close to an hour and at no point have either of you declared that you didn't love each other or that you didn't want to get married? Just sayin'." she held up the 'talk to the hand' signal.

They both stared at her and then at each other. Seung-Hwa reached out and held Jessica's hands between his own.

"Oh, for God's sake, just kiss her already!" Angelique called back to them as she headed to her room to give them some privacy.

***

Angelique's DNA test results were quietly submitted along with the required documentation. Her brother had chosen her Korean name, heavenly messenger, which was a shortened form of her first name from Angelique to Angel. She was recorded in the family registry as Min Cheon-Sa.

***

Her wedding date was set and arrangements made. She entrusted them to a wedding planner as she had absolutely no desire to have any part in it. She was thankful that there could be no honeymoon until after the drama was finished filming. Security had to be doubled at the studio and location sites as thousands of sasaeng gathered each day to get a glimpse of the happy couple. Netizens argued and took bets on whether or not the hasty date was because she was pregnant; others hated on her for landing such a catch. *Off Seoul Searching* once again dominated the internet.

EPISODE 14 – KEEPING THE HOME FIRES BURNING

Hyung-Joo let himself into his Cambridge, MA home. He had managed to complete most of his assignments electronically from the hospital so that he wasn't far behind in his classes. He would have one final set of projects in place of finals. After graduation he would put the house up for sale and return to Korea and start work as the President and CEO of LH Group. He would answer only to his father who was Chairman. It would remain like that until his father retired and he succeeded him.

He had wondered why he had been in Seoul in the middle of a semester. All of his memories leading up to the accident were missing. He didn't even remember traveling to his homeland at all. His father explained that he had been at the studio evaluating it for the purpose of a network acquisition. It made perfect sense but it was strange to have someone else telling you what you were doing and why you were doing it. It felt unnatural somehow.

The doctors told him that memory loss was normal with head injuries and that they had expected them to have returned within a few days. They admitted that the longer they didn't, the less likely they were to come back. He supposed that he would just have to learn to live with it.

He kicked off his shoes and wandered into the kitchen to look for something to eat. While his manservant had made sure that both the pantry and fridge were fully stocked, nothing seemed to strike his fancy. As he moved stuff around he came across a box of mint herbal teabags. He had the feeling that it was significant but couldn't understand why. He wasn't really all that fond of tea. He was frustrated that he often felt on the verge of recollection but nothing ever materialized. He imagined that eventually he would stop dwelling on it.

He wearily climbed the stairs to the second floor, dragging himself along with the aid of the handrail. It had been a very long day. He opened the double doors to his master bedroom suite. He stopped instantly. He stood motionless as he took in the mural on the largest wall.

It was a portrait of a young, beautiful girl reclining on a chaise lounge. She wore a strapless form fitting black taffeta gown. In her right hand she held a ramyun bowl; in her left a pair of chopsticks, dripping with noodles. Scattered across the coffee table and floor were empty boxes and wrappers from popular Korean snacks - pepero and choco heim. She was watching a caricature old-fashioned TV with a scene from *Secret Garden* decoupaged onto the wall where the screen would be.

Atop her head was a lopsided cartoonish three-pointed gold crown, each tip bearing a different colored jewel. Above her head were a series of thought clouds, each bearing a decoupaged scene from different KDramas.

In a heap on the chair situated kitty corner from her, was a marionette with his face. The wooden arms and legs were tangled with the string. The control bar was draped over the arm within easy reach.

Hyung-Joo grabbed the doorjamb but his grip wasn't firm enough for support. He fell to his knees as wave after wave of memories crashed over him with the brutal force of a tsunami.

EPISODE 15 – LIAR, LIAR, PANTS ON FIRE

Jessica and Seung-Hwa entered the courthouse on the appointed date and appointed time as instructed.

Seung-Hwa looked lovingly at his bride-to-be. He reached out and cupped her cheek in the palm of his hand. "I'm so very sorry."

"For what?" Jessica's voice was strained, wondering if he was getting cold feet.

"I know that this isn't how you imagined your wedding day would be." he said sadly. That wasn't just conjecture. He did know. His sister had told him. Multiple times.

Jessica took his hand from her cheek and stroked it lightly. "Eloping is romantic too." she told him.

Seung-Hwa placed the ring on her finger; Jessica did the same. They had chosen simple plain platinum bands.

Yo-Hyun and one of the court clerks signed the marriage certificate as witnesses. The registration form then received an official seal from the notary. Yo-Hyun took a picture of the couple holding the proof of their union and sent it to Angelique.

"That's it?" Jessica asked dubiously.

"I'm afraid so." Seung-Hwa responded sadly, apologizing again.

Jessica shrugged her shoulders. "You can spend the rest of your life making it up to me." She threw her arms around his neck and kissed him.

***

Angelique sat in the anteroom of the main ballroom of the Shilla hotel in her Victoria Swarovski wedding gown receiving well-wishing attendees and taking pictures. When her father entered, the room cleared.

He approached her and, as agreed, he showed her the text and photo that Yo-Hyun had sent to her handphone. She had stipulated as part of their agreement that the photo must be sent by Yo-Hyun to her handphone to be sure that no graphic editing had taken place.

She nodded and rose, hiked up her dress, and slipped her shoes back on. While she did so, Chairman Min turned off her handphone and slid it into his jacket pocket along with Seung-Hwa's and Jessica's powered down handphones. It had been his condition that the handphones of all parties be confiscated to be certain that there was no collusion amongst the trio.

What he had failed to show her were all the missed calls and texts from Lee Hyung-Joo which he had deleted from all three phones before blocking the caller's number on the lot of them.

***

Hyung-Joo endured the 17 hour flight from Boston to Incheon in his private suite onboard the Korean Airbus a380 wondering why in hell no one was responding to his messages.

***

Angelique took one final look into the mirror and smoothed some stray hairs back into place. Chairman Min held out his arm for her and she rested her arm atop his.

She grabbed her bouquet and said flatly, "Let's get this charade over with."

They both nodded and entered the venue.

***

Guests, who had been whispering among themselves at the absence of several key figures in the bride's life, most notably her brother, rose at the first notes of the Wedding March. All oohed and aahed at what a beautiful bride she made as Angelique smiled and nodded to many of her co-workers who had caught her eye during the procession.

While the Officient droned on about love and marriage and how fate and fortune had brought the pair before them together, Angelique and Ji-Tae faced each other, held each other's hands, and stared into each other's eyes.

Those gathered were deeply touched at how the couple only had eyes for each other. In truth, what they shared was their own private and collective hells.

This was no more the wedding that Angelique had planned than the one that her best friend had been stuck with. She was alone without friends or family on what should have been the most important day of her life. She mourned the loss of her first and true love. The only soul with whom she had any connection at his affair was the man in front of her. They had a bond for sure, precarious as it were, but could it be enough to share a lifetime? Angelique squeezed his hand tightly to both send and receive support.

Ji-Tae did not have the same reservations as his bride-to-be. He had always known that he wouldn't marry for love. It was the curse that was the birthright of every Chaebol. Yet, he too, had someone that he was leaving behind for the woman who stood before him. He mourned that loss as she did her own.

He couldn't miss the fact that she still wore her engagement ring. He knew that he would never replace the one who put it there in her heart. He also couldn't miss the fact that she flinched ever so slightly every time that there was a rustle in the audience. She was terrified that something would go wrong and that those that she cared about and that she was working so hard to protect, himself included, would suffer because of it.

Rather than return the squeeze of her hand, Ji-Tae worked to extricate himself from it. Angelique gripped even tighter, her eyes pleading for him not to let go. He felt her trembling in that grasp.

"I can't do this." he said in hushed tones, trying to untangle his hands from hers.

"Don't." she begged. "Think about everyone and everything you need to protect." she implored with every fiber of her being, relinquishing her hold on his fingertips and grabbing hold of his arms instead. "Jebal."

He placed his hands on her shoulders and pushed her away to arms length. "I am. And I'm starting with you." Then using his actor's training, pitched his voice so that it could be heard by all, "I love you Angelique Randolph for everything that you have done for me even when I didn't deserve it. But I can't marry you. I'm gay."

He was glad that he had held onto her because he had to lower her to the floor as her knees buckled and her legs gave way and she melted into the puddle of fabric that was her dress.

The guests who had started to realize that something was wrong, gasped in astonishment at the announcement and muttered amongst themselves as they saw themselves out. They pitied the poor bride who obviously, from her reaction, had no idea.

Ji-Tae left Angelique in the care of a few of her closer co-workers who had come up to console her. As he left the hall, he stopped for a moment before her father who had jumped to his feet in anger. "Go ahead and release your photos. I believe that I have you to thank for them." Then he left the building before he could get thrown out of his almost-father-in-law's hotel.

Angelique scanned the almost abandoned hall for her father with panic filled eyes. She knew if she couldn't convince him that this had not been staged that there would be hell to pay. She didn't see him anywhere. She brought her knees up, folded her arms across them, hung her head in them, and wailed, "Ji-Tae, what have you done?" Her friends patted her back to comfort her.

EPISODE 16 – FINAL EPISODE – SETTING THE WORLD ON FIRE

Seung-Hwa and Jessica knew that they would have missed the ceremony but they rushed as quickly as they could to the Shilla and hoped to be there to support Angelique during the reception. They let themselves in quietly so as to be as unobtrusive as possible. They knew that their absence would have been noted during the actual nuptials but had planned to blame traffic and car trouble. They were astounded to realize that none of their precautions had been necessary. They found Angelique alone, sitting at the desert table, and stuffing her face with dok, a traditional Korean wedding rice cake.

"Grab a fork!" she called to them across the hall.

After she had filled them in on what had transpired, Jessica helped her change out of her wedding dress and the trio headed out of the ballroom. They were aware of the whispering of the staff as they passed but ignored it. Angelique had already resigned herself to the fact that she would be a laughing stock and fuel for the gossipmongers for quite some time.

Seung-Hwa and Jessica had already made the decision to delay the honeymoon under the circumstances. They didn't even discuss it. They looked at each other and both knew that they couldn't leave Angelique at a time like this. That didn't stop Jessica from good-naturedly teasing her husband, "You'll have to make this up to me too. You're wracking up quite a tab there yeobo!"

They had decided that it would probably be safest to head back to the apartment. As they went to go down the stairs, Angelique noticed Hyung-Joo coming in the front entrance below. She stepped backward behind her brother so as not to be seen. She grabbed his coattails and buried her face in his back.

"I just can't deal with his indifference right now. I just can't. Not on top of everything else."

Seung-hwa took them out the back way.

***

***

Hyung-Joo had learned of the wedding from the reports on the TV screens at the airport. He grabbed a cab and went directly to the hotel. Once there, it was easy to discern what had happened. The lobby was abuzz with the news. Knowing Angelique as he did, he could now piece together what he had seen transpire on the studio lot and knew exactly why she had responded the way that she had. He raced to the ballroom but found it empty. He had missed her. He tried to call her again but it went straight to voicemail. He then tried Seung-Hwa and Jessica with the same results. What the hell was going on?

***

Yo-Hyun waited patiently and at a discreet distance while the group discussed their next course of action. His handphone vibrated in his pocket. He took it out and read the message from the corporate office.

"Pardon the interruption, sir, but I think that you should see this." he said, handing the phone to Seung-Hwa.

Seung-Hwa looked up at Yo-Hyun, concern etched on his face. No one had been able to reach him directly so the office had contacted his secretary in an attempt to locate him.

"This isn't good." he said to Yo-Hyun, and then explained to his wife and sister, "They have called an emergency meeting of the Board of Directors. It looks as if someone has been buying up small shares of stock using multiple shell companies and has accumulated enough support to attempt a takeover of Min Enterprises."

They gathered their belongings and headed out the door. Yo-Hyun ran ahead to pull the car around.

***

As they exited the building, Angelique in the lead, they saw Hyung-Joo alight from a taxi. She steeled herself for his aloofness and bowed her greeting. But as she straightened, she was surprised to find herself in his arms. He had pulled her into a fierce embrace, clinging to her desperately.

He whispered in her ear, "Woman, you have the most annoying habit of making me think that I have lost you. You're going to have to work on that."

Seung-Hwa slapped him on the back, "No time for that. I'll bring you up to speed in the car. Get in."

They piled into the sedan and Yo-Hyun pulled the vehicle out into the heavy afternoon rush-hour traffic.

***

When the five of them entered the conference room, Chairman Min, was huddled together with several stockholders. There was a distinct division in the room. Lines had been drawn and sides had been taken. They moved to the back; it was standing room only.

The door opened again and a statuesque, smartly dressed, platinum blonde waltzed into the chamber. She looked around, saw Angelique in the back, and waved.

"Eomma?" Angelique asked incredulously, her mouth gaping wide.

Over the girls heads, Hyung-Joo and Seung-Hwa looked at each other and mouthed the same word in the same tone. They whipped their heads back around.

"How dare you show your face in my boardroom? Get out!" bellowed Chairman Min.

"Nice to see you again too, Hoonie." Danielle said with a sweet southern smile; her drawl dripping like honey. She moved to the podium and addressed the assembled group, "I make a motion for the immediate dismissal of the current Chairman."

It was then that he realized that she, impossible as it was, was the threat that he was facing. Chairman Min did a quick calculation.

"As I see it, at best, you are still many votes short of being able to win that motion, even if you could get a second."

Yo-Hyun, who had been standing at his normal position, slightly behind and to the left of Seung-Hwa, moved forward to be at his side. He faced him, and his arms slid down his legs as he doubled in half in a deep and formal bow.

"My sincerest apologies. I hope that you all can find it in your hearts to forgive me." Then he straightened and called out, "I second the motion."

He walked forward, approached the podium, reached into his jacket, and handed a packet to Danielle Randolph. She opened the manilla envelope and removed the proxies.

Danielle Randolph cocked her head and looked coyly at Min Dong-Hoon. "I think not." Then the smile she had worn since her entrance faded. "Never," she punctuated the word, "underestimate a momma bear protecting her cub."

Chairman Min was both furious and amused at his former lover's gall. He fumed, "You can't possibly think that even those who would vote for my dismissal would put that bastard child of yours in my place."

Murmurs of assent circulated around the room.

She threw her head back and laughed uproariously. She smiled slyly, "I have no intention of throwing *our* child to the hyenas. I nominate Min Seung-Hwa as Chairman."

She stared at him, daring him to object. Min Dong-Hoon stormed from the boardroom.

She looked at Seung-Hwa, who was still reeling at the events that had just taken shape, and continued, "But, puh-leaze, for the love of all that is holy, put her in charge of RG Entertainment because I am sick to death of listening to her rant about how shabbily they treat their artists."

Angelique snapped her head in her brother's direction. "We own RG Entertainment?" she hauled off and backhanded him hard across the chest. Jessica mirrored her on his other side.

"What the hell did I do?" he asked perplexed.

Hyung-Joo snickered, "Welcome to *my* world."

***

After the meeting had been adjourned and the crowd thinned, Danielle Randolph made her way to them.

She looked directly at Hyung-Joo and gave him a warning. "You will find yourself in a similar position tomorrow. Be ready."

She hugged her daughter tightly and, when she had released her, she addressed them collectively, "Your lives are truly your own now. Remember the lessons that you have learned and live them well."

***

Later, when they were alone in the apartment, Hyung-Joo turned to Angelique. "Which world do you want to live in?"

She stood on tip-toes and threw her arms around his neck. She adjusted the three-pointed crown atop her head that few besides she could see. With a big smile and sparkling eyes, she answered, "KDrama Land, of course!"

He had meant did she want to stay in Korea or return to the States but she had given him her answer in the way that was all her own. He noticed was there was no longer any trace of the haunted look that had lurked there.

He lifted her up into the air and spun her around in the air as he had done when she had accepted his proposal. She beamed down at him as lovingly as she did that day. At that time, he had told her that he didn't know exactly when she had brought him into her world, but he knew that he didn't want to live anywhere else. Especially if it meant living there without her. He still felt the same.

Hers would never be an easy world to live in. It was tumultuous at best, tempestuous at worst. But, he thought that he could learn to circumnavigate it.

When he set her down, he pulled her close and looked adoringly into her eyes.

"Saranghaeyo." he confessed his love for her.

"Saranghaeyo, Oppa." she replied.

"And saranghaeyo Ji Chang-Wook Oppa and Lee Jae-Wook Oppa and Cha Eun-Woo Oppa and …" he teased her about her fickleness regarding her KPop idols and KDrama leads.

She placed her fingers lightly over his lips to hush him, "Just one 'Oppa'. Lee Hyung-Joo Oppa."

Hyung-Joo counted to three, waiting for the hiccup. When it didn't come, he lowered his face to hers and kissed her.

끝 kkeut (The End)

A NOTE TO MY READERS

My eternal thanks and gratitude to you all for joining Angelique on her journey through KDrama Land. I hope that you have enjoyed the trip. It has certainly been my pleasure being your host and guide.

For those of you who like happy endings, please, do **NOT** turn the page. Let Episode 16 be your final episode and how you last remember our female lead.

For those of you who like the types of KDramas that have an end that still leaves you with questions and wanting more, fully aware that it may never come, I offer you an Easter Egg. Please, read on.

Either way, you have been warned.

EASTER EGG – GRACE UNDER FIRE

Slender fingers with long, tapered, meticulously manicured nails painted a bright cherry red, caressed the feathers of the three darts she held in her hand. She raised them, took aim, and rapidly fired them off, one after the other, at three separate boards. Each flew true and hit their targets squarely between the eyes – photos of Lee Hyung-Joo, Min Seung-Hwa, and Angelique Randolph.

With poise and grace, Park Eun-Chae crossed the room and struck a pose on her Louis XV divan. She picked up her champagne flute and raised it to her lips leaving prints on the glass that matched the color of her nails. Reclining lazily, she plotted her revenge.

끝 kkeut (The End)